I0521500

NO WAY OUT

Love & Lies Book 2

Alex Strong

Red Dahlia Publishing

NO WAY OUT

Cover Art © konradbak/BortN66/fotolia
Cover Design by J.P. Irons

ISBN: 978-0-9913614-8-9

I dedicate this book to my mom. I know she would have been my biggest fan.

CHAPTER ONE

If Aaron Wells had to listen to Aleksandr Morozov's wife talk about her dress for this upcoming event much longer, he was afraid he might have to stab himself with his fork. And that would draw attention to himself, which would be bad.

"Shall I wear the blue dress or the black dress?" Mrs. Morozov asked her husband.

"You'll wear the blue one," said Morozov from the booth directly behind Aaron. He was surprised by the definite, answer and Aaron realized his wife had been asking for his decision, not his opinion.

Aaron had been sitting in this café almost every weekday morning for the past two weeks, hoping to glean some info on Ukrainian mob head Aleksandr Morozov. But so far he knew nothing more than he did when he asked for the assignment. He needed to change his approach and get something soon or his supervisors would pull him off the case.

"Are you ready to go?" said Morozov.

There was a pause before his wife answered. "If it's okay with you, I think I'll walk over to Nordstrom and find some jewelry to go with the dress if you've decided on the blue one."

Aaron rolled his eyes.

"Suit yourself," Aleksandr said as he stood. "Call Ryan when you're ready to go home."

"Of course."

Aleksandr walked by, and Aaron's gaze followed him out the door. He was about to get up himself when Clara Morozov slid onto the bench across from him. *Shit.*

"Can I help you?" he asked.

"So which one are you?" she said. "FBI? ATF? DEA, perhaps?"

"I'm sorry?"

"Because I can help you."

What the hell was this woman playing at?

"Listen lady," he said, "I don't know who you think I am, but you are clearly—"

"Cut the bullshit," she said, "I know exactly what you are. Well, not exactly. I haven't decided which agency. But you should know Aleksandr is taunting you by sitting in this stupid café every day and giving you absolutely nothing."

[2]

Her mesmerizing green eyes never wavered as she spoke, and Aaron stared at her, wondering what to think of Mrs. Morozov. Was this a trap? Or was this the in that he needed?

"And what makes you so sure that I'm here because of your husband?" he asked, still trying to decide if should trust her.

"Because I heard him talking about it on the phone," she said. "Someone warned him."

"Fuck," Aaron muttered. Then he shook his head. "I don't think you realize what you're trying to do. But I can tell you it's not a good idea."

Clara's hands shot across the table and wrapped around one of his. He looked at it and frowned, disgusted by the ostentatious rock on one of her long fingers.

"I'm sorry," she said, pulling her hands away. "But I don't think *you* realize that you'll never be able to touch my husband. You *need* me. Please."

It was the plea at the end that really got to Aaron. But he still wasn't sure how to handle this.

"Meet me tomorrow at two o'clock," she said. "In Bellevue Park." She got up and left without waiting for his response.

***

As Clara stepped out of the café, she could feel her whole body start to tremble and tried to control it. She needed to look calm and collected, at least until

[3]

she was out of sight. She took a couple of deep, ragged breaths and headed towards the mall two blocks away. If she didn't come home with something, Aleksandr would be suspicious. The whole time she tried not to think about what her husband would do to her if he even suspected what she was attempting. Then again, wasn't she already living on borrowed time?

***

The minute Clara walked out the door, Aaron sent an encrypted message and waited. Twenty minutes later his supervisor from Section Four, the clandestine operation he worked for, came striding in and sat down where Clara had made her plea earlier.

"What's so important that we had to meet in person?" Gavin Maxwell asked.

"You're never going to believe who just approached me," said Aaron.

"Let me guess. Aleksandr Morozov himself," Gavin said in jest. "He wants to do the right thing and turn himself in."

"Close," Aaron said as Gavin filled his coffee cup from the carafe. "His wife. Clara."

"You can't be serious," Gavin said, no longer paying attention to what he was doing.

Aaron grabbed the pitcher from him before the coffee spilled over. "I am. And she informs me that someone warned Morozov about me."

"Do you think she's telling the truth?" Gavin asked.

"She's right, isn't she? And we still don't know how Morozov got Jackson's name. It'd be safe to assume he got the intel on me the same way."

Gavin ran a hand through his jet black hair. "We need to find where this leak is coming from."

"Agreed. But what do we do about Morozov in the meantime?" asked Aaron.

Gavin took a sip from his mug without saying anything.

"I really wanted to take this bastard down once and for all," Aaron said. "But I can't do that if he's a step ahead of us every time."

"Take his wife up on her offer."

"You're joking."

"No, I'm not," said Gavin. "There isn't much we can do from our end if we don't know who the mole is. She could be the break we've been looking for. She'll be able to get into places we never could."

"I don't think it's a good idea bringing a civilian in on this," Aaron said, shaking his head.

"It rarely is, but give me a better plan. Or, let me replace you with someone who is willing to work with her."

Aaron narrowed his eyes at Gavin. "Fine. Does this at least mean I can move back into my own home?"

Gavin shook his head. "I want whoever's talking to

Morozov to think that you're working the case as originally planned. I'll talk to Director Rollins and we'll keep Mrs. Morozov's involvement between the three of us, and let the mole think you're just hitting dead ends. And no information over the phones. Just in case."

Aaron sighed, leaning back against the seat. He hated the overpriced studio apartment he was renting here in Bellevue. But he'd lived in worse conditions for a case before.

"It's a plan then," he said.

Gavin nodded. "It's a plan."

***

Several people were out enjoying the sunshine as Aaron wandered Bellevue Park, looking for Clara Morozov. She had told him to meet here, but hadn't been specific where in the two hundred acre park she wanted to meet. He was pulling his cap down closer to his sunglasses when a woman sitting on one of the benches with dark copper hair caught his attention and he knew it must be her. She was wearing dark sunglasses and a striped silk scarf, reading a book.

He sat down on the bench next to her.

"I was worried you wouldn't come," she said without lifting her eyes from the thick book.

"I almost didn't."

"What is it that you need me to do?" she asked.

"Are you sure you want to do this?" he said. "I

can't imagine your husband would take kindly to you betraying him."

She finally looked up from the book but still didn't look in his direction. He followed her gaze to children running around a playground across the park.

"No, I imagine he wouldn't."

"Then why risk it?" Aaron asked, looking back at her again.

"I have my reasons," she said, turning to look at him finally, but he couldn't read her eyes from beneath the sunglasses. "Now what do you need me to do?"

Aaron let it go. "I need a serial number off the back of his phone. It would be located under the battery. Do you think you can handle that?"

Clara's smooth forehead wrinkled into a frown. "He rarely leaves that phone out of his sight."

"But as his wife, I'm sure you could find an opportunity."

"I'll figure something out." But the frown didn't leave her face.

"If you can, snap a picture of it and then text it, along with his phone number, to this number." He handed her a business card for Alliance Security Systems.

"Tim Hanson," she said. "Is that your name?"

"It's an alias," he said. "If you call that number, though, you'll get a voice recording for Tim Hanson in sales. In case it should fall into the wrong hands."

She nodded.

"You can leave a message with that number as well," he added. "If you ever need to get a hold of me."

She ran a finger across the card with reverence before putting it into a zippered pocket of her white Prada bag.

"So I get you the number off his phone and then is that it? Will it be enough?" she asked.

"It will be a start. I should be able to clone his phone and we'll have to see what info I can get off of it."

"I see." She looked at her watch and stood. "I should get going." Clara started to walk away, but then turned around. "Are you ever going to tell me your name? Or should I call you Tim?"

"Just call me Aaron."

"Well, I'm Clara. But you probably already knew that."

Aaron nodded. She stood there, and Aaron wondered if she was wanting him to say something more, but then she finally nodded as well, and he watched her delicate frame walk away.

***

It had been over an hour since Clara had found herself wide awake, but now she pretended to be asleep as her husband climbed out of bed and into the shower. This was the only time during the day that his phone would not be on him. It had already been three days since she'd promised Aaron she could get the numbers. It was now or never.

His Blackberry was sitting right there on his nightstand and she slid across the bed toward it with her own cell phone in hand. She pulled the back off, and in the pale light spilling from the bathroom, could just make out the numbers Aaron told her to look for. The first picture she took was too dark to be usable so she turned on her flash, only this time it was too bright and a majority of the numbers were washed out.

"Dammit," she quietly cursed. She turned Aleksandr's bedside lamp on and held the phone up to it to make a third, and this time successful, attempt.

The water stopped and Clara's heart pounded in her chest. She turned the light off so as not to attract Aleksandr's attention while putting the battery back in. But the phone wasn't powering back up. Assuming she put it in wrong, she pulled it out and tried again, this time with better luck, but now the back wouldn't go on and her sweating hands were making the task all that much harder. Through the crack in the door she could see Aleksandr at the mirror, shaving, and she prayed with all her might that he couldn't see her struggle in the dark. Why couldn't she get the damn cover back on? Then she felt the tab and realized she was trying to put it in upside down. She flipped it and it snapped into place. She looked up in panic, worried that he had heard the noise, but it had only been loud to her.

Clara replaced the phone on the nightstand and settled in once again beneath the covers, trying to even out her breathing. All in all, it had been a simple enough task, but she felt as though she had just survived diffusing a bomb. Now she just had to wait for the right opportunity to send it to Aaron.

***

Aaron was in his apartment making a sandwich when the text from Clara came in.

"Nicely done," he said aloud. The past few days with no word had gotten him worried that she had chickened out. Or that something had gone horribly wrong.

He called her phone and she picked up almost immediately.

"Was it okay?" she asked. "Can you make out the numbers?"

"Perfect," he said. "When can you meet me?"

"I'm not sure. Can I call you back?"

"Of course. And Clara…"

"Yes?"

"Make sure you erase the photo and text off your phone," he said.

[10]

"I already did."

"Good. Call me when you know."

The line went dead without any response from her end.

Aaron sat down at the counter and worked on activating the clone. Aaron probably would have been able to get the serial number himself eventually, but not only did Clara just save him a lot of time, there was less suspicion this way.

***

It had been almost a week, but Clara finally left Aaron a message saying to meet him on the second level of the city library. He was starting to get the impression that Morozov kept a pretty tight leash on his wife. He supposed one had to be a bit of a control freak to be the head of a family crime organization.

Aaron found her reading at a table and caught the title when she closed it as he sat down. *Anna Karenina* by Tolstoy.

"Not exactly light reading," he said, and was caught off guard by her smile.

"No, but it's sad and beautiful at the same time." She pushed the book aside. "Were you able to get what you needed?"

"Yes and no," he said. "So far I've been able to compile a list of contacts. Mostly people we knew he was associated with, but there were a couple surprises, including a senator. Morozov doesn't give

[11]

a lot of details during his phone calls."

Clara sighed. "No. Since the death of his father and brothers, he's been extremely cautious. That's why you need me."

Aaron nodded. He knew perfectly well that this woman was putting herself in grave danger by helping him, but there hadn't been any other options. Over the years, no one had been able to take down any of the major players in the family. And after Morozov made it personal last year, Aaron was determined to do what no one else had been able to do. He reminded himself that she had approached him, not the other way around.

"Why are you doing this?" he asked. "What do you get out of it? If your husband goes to jail, do you get all the money to yourself?" The second the words escaped Aaron, he knew he had misread the whole situation.

Clara's expression turned icy, almost angry. "Do you really think that the government or whoever takes my husband down will let me take a penny of his blood money?" She turned her gaze to the window behind him, and her expression softened just ever so slightly. "No. All I ask is to be able to walk away."

Aaron could see something else behind her green eyes, something she wasn't willing to share. But it didn't take a mind reader to know that this woman was living in fear of her husband. Which only led to more questions in Aaron's mind, but he knew now was not the time nor the place to ask them. Or if he even had a right to ask them. Clara Morozov was nothing more than an asset, and Aaron would do well to keep that in mind.

"What is it that you need me to do for you now?" she asked.

"Your husband alluded to a container arriving next month. No details of course, but it obviously can't be anything good—probably drugs or guns. Do you think you could get me more info on it?"

Clara hesitated. "That would be in his office if he has anything written down. Even I don't have access to it."

"But could you find a way?"

"I— I don't know."

"At the moment, that's all I have to work with. See what you can get, and if something else turns up, I'll let you know."

She nodded.

"You still have the card with my number?"

Her head shook. "I memorized it and threw the card away. It was still too risky."

"I understand," he said. "Call me if you come up with anything."

***

Clara walked into the expansive Mediterranean-style home on Meydenbaeur Bay that she shared with her husband. In the bedroom she found him putting a pistol into the safe and she shuddered. There was only one reason he ever pulled it out. Aleksandr locked the safe and swung the wedding portrait back over it. She looked at the picture and her heart ached over the genuine smiles on their faces. How naive she had been.

"How was the library?" Aleksandr asked.

"Fine," she said and tossed a book on the bed. Clara knew his interest was only to confirm that she had actually gone there. Not that she could have gotten away with a lie. He had Ryan, her driver, check in with him throughout the day on her whereabouts.

"Ukrainian Heritage Cooking?" he said. "What do you need a book for? Let my mother teach you."

"I think your mother would do more criticizing than teaching," said Clara.

"She has high expectations."

"Then why do you insist on me making traditional fare when she comes over for dinner? It's always a disaster."

Aleksandr cupped her chin. "Because that is what a good Morozov does."

Clara jerked her face from his hand and immediately hoped he was in a good mood.

"But I'm not Ukrainian," she said.

[14]

Aleksandr shrugged and walked out of the room. The conversation was over.

***

Another week had gone by with no word from Clara, and Aaron was trying not to worry. The task he had given her was going to be more difficult and require more finesse. But he hated not knowing if she simply needed more time or had been caught. Several times he picked up the phone thinking he should call her, then realized that was not a smart move — it could put her in jeopardy if she wasn't already.

Aaron wandered the park and library from time to time hoping to run into her, but nothing. The only consolation was that Morozov wasn't giving any indication in his phone calls that anything was wrong. Aaron was just going to have to sit tight for a while longer.

***

Clara was in the front room reading when someone rang the doorbell.

"I'll get it," she called out, walking to the front door.

"Mrs. Morozov," said the man on the other side. "Always a pleasure to see you."

His gold-capped sneer sent waves of revulsion through her.

"Peter." Clara made no attempt to hide her disdain for her husband's courier. She was certain that his fear of Aleksandr was the only thing keeping his hands off of her.

"Mr. Morozov asked to see me," he said.

"I will get him. Wait here."

She went upstairs and knocked on the door of Aleksandr's office. The phone was pressed to his ear as usual when he opened the door.

"What is it?" he asked.

"Peter's here," she said. "He says you called for him."

Without answering, he went over to his desk and grabbed a package, then walked out past Clara. She was shocked that he hadn't closed the door behind him and realized this may be her one opportunity. Just a quick glance to see if anything jumped out at her.

She rushed over to the desk, listening for Aleksandr returning. Where should she start? The desk was a mess, papers everywhere. Aleksandr knew computers could be hacked, so he put everything down with pen.

And then she saw it. A shipping invoice. It was mostly covered, but she could see a country of origin and date. She started to carefully lift the paper over it, but then she heard Peter's car tearing out of the driveway and knew she needed to get out of there.

She had just stepped out into the hall when Aleksandr's head appeared over the landing. At first

[16]

he looked confused, but then his expression changed to anger.

"What are you doing?" he asked as he finished climbing the stairs.

"Nothing." Could he hear the quivering in her voice? Oh god, she hoped not.

"Were you in my office?"

Clara crossed her arms. "Of course not. Why would I?"

Aleksandr's lip started to twitch, and she was sure she had done it now. Whether it was the tone in her voice or the fact that he didn't believe her didn't matter. She held her breath and prepared for the worst.

The phone in his hand starting ringing and she jumped. He narrowed his cold gray eyes at her before answering the phone and slamming the door behind him.

***

Clara ran to her bedroom, unplugged her phone from the charger, and locked herself in the bathroom. She slumped against the door and let her body slide to the floor. Would Aleksandr cool off? Or would he just come at her later? She could only stay locked in this bathroom so long.

She dialed Aaron's number, but she had to take several deep breaths before hitting the call button.

"Alliance Security Systems, this is Tim," said a

voice on the other end.

"Aaron?" she whispered. She had been expecting the recorded message.

"Clara?" he said. "Are you okay?"

"Yes." She continued to whisper. Then she realized it might be smart to turn the water on in case she didn't hear Aleksandr coming again. "I found an invoice. I think it's coming from Hong Kong on September 19th."

"Got it," he said. "Clara, are you sure you're all right?"

She fought back the tears as she thought of what might be waiting for her. "I will be."

"When can we meet again?"

"I don't know yet. I'll call you." And she hung up the phone.

***

Aaron put the phone on the counter and resisted the urge to call her back. She was clearly shaken, and he wondered what this information had just cost her.

He did his best to push it out of his mind and focus on the new information. A database search showed there was only one ship from Hong Kong due to arrive in Seattle on the date Clara had just given him, which narrowed things down. However, it was still a pool of about five hundred containers. He had four weeks to figure out which container, what exactly was in it, and how to tie it directly to Aleksandr

Morozov. No problem. Aaron was sure he had worked with tighter deadlines.

***

It was a relief the next day when Clara left him a message telling him to meet her at the library again.

"Must be your favorite place," he said as he sat down, noticing that she was wearing a scarf again. This one was printed with blue and green swirly patterns. He had a feeling the silk scarf cost more than his whole outfit combined.

"My driver, Ryan, won't follow me into the building," she said. "He claims to be allergic to reading. He says just the thought of all these books makes him itch."

"You have your own driver?" Aaron asked.

"Well, that's the official title. However, handler would be a more apt job description."

More evidence of Morozov's controlling nature, Aaron decided. He was getting a sense of why Clara was so desperate to hand her husband over to the authorities. He felt a tinge of sadness for the beautiful woman sitting across from him. He also felt a lot of admiration for the balls she had, taking on the man that no one else could touch.

"Did the info I give you help?" she asked, jarring Aaron from his thoughts.

"It narrows down my search," he said, and she nodded. The scarf around her throat shifted with the movement, and he caught a glimpse of discoloration beneath it.

"What's that?" he asked.

"It's nothing," she said, not meeting his eye as she readjusted the scarf. "Is there anything else you need me to help with?"

Aaron frowned but decided to drop it. For now.

"There *is* one thing," he said.

"What?" she asked.

"I need you to take pictures whenever possible."

Her eyes went wide.

"Even if we find this container, I need indisputable proof connecting it to your husband."

"What about a gun?" she asked.

"What kind of gun?"

"It doesn't have anything to do with this container you're looking for, but what if I could get you the gun he uses?"

Now Aaron's eyes got big. "You have access to his gun?"

"Well, no, not exactly. But I know where he keeps it. If you had it, could you tie it to people he's killed with it?"

Aaron's thumb traced his jawline as he considered this new info. "I suppose. Do you know for sure he has used it?"

Clara began nervously rubbing her left arm with her right hand. "I know the only reason he ever pulls it out of the bedroom safe is with the intent to use it. Though even that isn't very often. He doesn't get his hands dirty if he can help it."

"Do you know who he's killed?"

She shook her head.

"So you don't even know for sure if the bodies have been found," he said, "if there are cold cases waiting for this kind of break."

She shook her head again. "I'm sorry."

"Don't be sorry," he told her. "This is still good to know. It could be the nail in the coffin. I just wouldn't risk it if we aren't sure it will link him to other crimes."

Clara's phone started vibrating from her purse. She pulled it out and Aaron was barely able to hear her words.

"You need to leave now."

He stood up and moved into the stacks.

"Yes, I am here," he heard her say. "Where are you?"

Through the books Aaron could see Clara stand up and look over the railing to the first floor. She slipped the phone back into her bag and walked down the stairs.

CHAPTER TWO

Clara could feel the color rising in her cheeks as she walked towards her husband. Did he know? Did he suspect?

"What are you doing here?" she asked, forcing a smile as he kissed her cheek. A good sign, she decided. "I thought you were headed to Vegas."

"Things are delayed," he said, leading her out the front door, "so I decided to leave in the morning. Ryan told me you were here and I wanted to take my wife out to dinner."

"How sweet," she said, feeling her heart return to a normal rate. "Did you have somewhere special in mind?"

"How about Daniel's? We haven't been there in a while."

"Sounds good to me," she said. She climbed into

the car, one of Aleksandr's hired muscles sat in the front seat.

At the restaurant, the hostess led them to a back table by the corner windows.

"Find anything good at the library today?" Aleksandr asked.

Clara remembered Aaron rubbing his chin only minutes earlier and was surprised to find herself wondering what those fingers would feel like over her skin.

"Not today," she said, squashing the image from her mind.

"No more cook books."

Clara crinkled her nose. "I gave up."

"Good," said Aleksandr. "It was nonsense."

"Then what hobby do you suggest I take up?" she asked.

He frowned. "What do you need a hobby for?"

"Because I'm bored," she said with a sigh.

"Then have a baby. That'll cure your boredom quickly."

Clara bit her tongue, fighting back all the words that she knew would only make things worse.

***

After Aaron was sure that Clara did not leave under duress, he headed back to his apartment.

That was close. Far too close. What if Morozov had come upstairs without calling first? He shook his

[23]

head. Fortunately that was not what happened, but he knew he couldn't contact her again without risking exposure.

***

Early the next morning Aaron's phone started ringing and he knew it was Clara, but he hesitated answering it. What if it was Morozov checking the number? He decided to let it go to voicemail. Clara said she had tossed the card, but what if….

It stopped ringing, and the most painful twenty seconds passed before the voicemail alert popped up. He listened to Clara telling him to call her back.

"Is everything all right?" he asked when she answered.

"I'm fine," she said. "But yesterday was close. I can't imagine if he had found us. Lucky he called first."

"I know, I was thinking the same thing."

"God, I feel like I'm having an affair or something."

"Something tells me that he'd be just as upset with what you're really doing," he said.

"True."

"Where is he now?" Aaron asked.

"He left for Vegas an hour ago," she said. "I'm currently locked in the bathroom. Ryan is downstairs playing babysitter until he gets back."

"You don't have to do this, you know. You can back out anytime."

"And do what? Just sit here waiting? And hoping?"

"I just don't want to see you get hurt." The words surprised Aaron. Did he really just say them?

Only silence on the other end.

"Clara, are you still there?"

She sniffed. "Yeah, I'm here. Sorry. It's just, um…I should probably go. I'll call you if I find anything useful."

"Clara—" But she had already ended the call.

***

Clara was slumped against the wall of her bathroom again. She placed her head on her knees and continued crying, still gripping the phone.

This was ridiculous. Why was she crying over Aaron saying he didn't want to see her get hurt? Maybe because it was the nicest thing anyone had said to her in a very long time. Or, maybe, it was because the tone of his voice made it sound genuine.

One thing was for sure, though. Sitting here crying on the bathroom floor was not going to help her get free of Aleksandr. She stood up, splashed some water on her face, and freshened her makeup. Tonight she was getting into his office.

***

By nine o'clock that evening, Clara was buzzing. It was time to put her plan in action.

Nine o'clock rolled around and she felt the time was right. She went into the kitchen and cracked open a bottle of syrah.

"I'm pouring myself a glass of wine," she called out to Ryan, who was flipping through an automotive magazine out on the balcony. "Would you like one?"

"Sure," he said. "That would be great, Mrs. Morozov."

She poured two glasses, but in one she added an oxycodone tablet that she had crushed up earlier that day. She swirled the glass and joined Ryan on the balcony looking out over the bay.

"I wonder how much longer this warm weather will last," she said, handing him a glass and sitting in the chair next to his.

"I know," he said. "With fall just around the corner, I'm sure the rain will start soon."

It was hard for Clara not to stare as he took a drink. Would he taste it?

"How long have you worked for us now, Ryan?"

"Almost four months, I think."

Four months since Aleksandr had stripped her of what little freedom she'd had. Clara took a sip, and he followed suit.

"Don't you ever wish you could do something besides just drive me around and look after my wellbeing when my husband is away?"

Ryan shrugged and took another drink before answering.

Good boy.

"It's not so bad. The pay is good, and you're a very nice person to work for."

"You're too sweet," she said with a smile. "But don't you want to move up in the ranks someday? Perhaps take on more responsibility?"

Another swig. Ryan was clearly not comfortable with this topic.

"I suppose. I mean sure. But at least working for you comes with less...risk."

"That is true," she said, resting her chin on her knuckles. "Well, if you ever decide you want to try something different, I promise to put in a good word with Aleksandr."

"I appreciate that, ma'am." He punctuated it with one last swig, finishing off the glass.

This was better than Clara had hoped. Hopefully it wouldn't be long now.

"Would you like me to refresh your glass?" she asked.

"No, I shouldn't. Thank you, though," he said. "But I think I'll grab a glass of water." He started to get up, but Clara stopped him.

"Let me get it for you." She grabbed his empty wine glass. "I have to take this in anyway. Mr. Morozov is very particular about how the stemware is washed."

"Thank you," he said with a gentle, almost pitying smile.

Clara took her time washing the wine glass and getting his water. When she returned to the balcony, Ryan was staring out over the bay. She handed him the water and he thanked her.

"You know," he said, "I think I might turn in for the night. I'm feeling kinda tired. Do you mind?"

"Go right ahead," she told him. "I know where to find you if I need anything."

"Good night, Mrs. Morozov." And he stood, taking the water with him.

"Good night, Ryan." She watched him head downstairs to the guest room he used when Aleksandr was out of town.

***

Once Ryan was out of sight, Clara closed up the French doors and set the alarm. She was pretty sure her husband wasn't coming home anytime that night, but just in case he had another surprise for her, at least the disarm beep would alert her. She couldn't risk being caught again.

She heard the water running in the bathroom downstairs and knew the next step would be Ryan crawling into bed and passing out soon after. But just to be sure, she sat on the stairs without moving for the next ten minutes. When no other sounds came from the downstairs, Clara ran up to the garage and located Aleksandr's old lock-picking kit. It was a miracle he still had it. She guessed he held onto it for sentimental reasons since he hadn't needed to pick a lock in years.

She went back downstairs and kneeled in front of his office door. Aleksandr probably never thought that when he taught Clara how to pick the lock to his family's restaurant, it would come back to bite him in the ass. She had never understood why he wanted to break in when he could have easily gotten a key, but it had been thrilling nonetheless. It had also made the sex they would have in the kitchen feel that much more forbidden.

But Clara pushed these memories out as she focused on the lock in front of her now. She was just starting to worry she would never get it open when the pin clicked. She was in.

She flipped on the light and pulled the phone out of her pocket, prepared to document everything she found. But her heart sank when the light spilled over the scene. All the papers that had littered his desk earlier were gone.

Maybe he just cleaned up, she thought. But a quick look through the cabinets and drawers showed that it was all gone. A couple manuals and notebooks sat on the shelves, but not a shred of anything incriminating.

Clara sat down at the desk, and for the second time that day, started crying.

***

When Aaron's phone started ringing just after ten p.m., he knew something was wrong.

"Clara, what is it?" he answered, abandoning all protocol.

"It's gone," she cried into the phone, "It's all gone!"

"What's gone?" he said. "Where are you?"

"I broke into Aleksandr's office—"

"You what?"

"—and all his papers are gone. He's cleaned out his desk."

"Weren't you in there before?" he asked.

"Yes, but only for a second. That's how I found the shipping info."

"Does he know it was you?"

"He suspected," she said. "I made it out just before he got back."

"He got spooked."

"Shit! Shit, shit, shit!"

"What is it? Is Aleksandr home?" asked Aaron.

"No, there's a camera in here! Shit! Aaron, what do I do?"

His heart pounded. They *were* fucked. He knew he should never have let her get involved.

***

Clara panicked when Aaron didn't immediately answer.

"Are you still there?" she asked. "Tell me what to do!"

"Was there always a camera?" he said.

"I don't know. I don't think so." She didn't remember seeing it the last time she was in here. Wouldn't Aleksandr have reacted if he had seen her on tape snooping?

"This must be new," she said. "But what does it matter? He has it now and when he watches the footage it will clearly show me breaking in."

"Is it transmitting wirelessly, or do you see a hard drive for it anywhere?"

Clara got up and poked around the shelves. "I doubt he would go wireless. He's paranoid about being hacked." She opened a cabinet. "I think I just found the hard drive. But now what?"

"Then we will just have to make you disappear from the footage," he said.

"How?" she asked.

"Well, it's not something I can talk you through over the phone, so I'll have to come to you."

"I don't know if that's a good idea," she said.

"I know, but what other choice do we have?"

Clara knew he was right but said nothing.

"Is Ryan still there?" he asked.

"Yes, but he's out for the night."

"Are you sure?"

"Yes," she said. "I drugged him."

"You *drugged* him?"

Clara could hear the worry in his voice.

"Relax," she said. "I just slipped a little oxycodone in his wine. He'll probably wake up tomorrow from the best sleep of his life."

"So in one night you have managed to drug Ryan and break into your husband's office."

This time Clara wasn't sure if it was awe or disbelief she detected in his voice. Perhaps both.

"It's been an interesting day," she told him. "Fine, you'll have to come over. But we have to be very careful."

***

Ten minutes later, Clara was letting Aaron in through the garage side door, and when he saw her puffy red eyes and tear-stained face, he had to restrain from pulling her into his arms and telling her it was going to be all right.

Get a grip on yourself, Wells.

"That was quick," she said. "You must be close."

"I'm at the apartments on Second and One-twelfth," he said.

"Oh. And you're sure no one saw you?" she asked.

"I'm a professional," he reminded her.

"I know, it's just…"

"I know," he said. "Let's get to work so I can get out of here."

She led him to the office where her kit was still sitting on the floor.

"Where did you learn to pick a lock?" he asked.

Clara was full of surprises.

"Long story. Here's the DVR."

Aaron pulled the iMac out of his backpack and hooked it up to the humming machine. He frowned.

"We're going to have to turn all the lights off, including the hall light," he said. "It's going to have to be seamless that this room is in darkness."

Clara nodded and started turning off all the lights while Aaron dimmed the brightness of his screen as much as could and still be able to use it. Success. He moved around a little to make sure his motions wouldn't be visible and then got to work patching the footage together and adjusting the time stamp. It wasn't going to hold up to the scrutiny of an experienced video tech, but Aaron just needed Morozov to believe nothing out of the ordinary had happened. Chances are he would just fast forward through it looking for any suspicious activity.

When he was sure it was as flawless as he was going to make it, Aaron disconnected and slowly moved out of the office.

"Would you care to do the honors?" Aaron asked when the door was shut.

"Oh no, my skills are rusty. It took me forever to get the thing unlocked."

Within seconds he had the door secure.

"I'm so sorry," Clara said as they walked back towards the garage. "I really made a mess of things, didn't I?"

Aaron stopped and put his hands on her shoulders.

"Don't be so hard on yourself," he said, staring into her beautiful green eyes. "It wasn't anything we couldn't handle. You saw an opportunity and took it. Quite brilliantly, I might add." Clara continued to look up at him, and he couldn't remember the last time he had wanted to kiss someone so badly. It was time to step away from her.

"But what do we do now?" she asked. "If he's moved everything off-site, how will I get access to it?"

"I'm not sure yet, but we'll figure something out. We should lay low though. It's obvious he's suspicious."

Clara opened the door for him and surprised him by kissing his cheek.

"Thank you," she said. Aaron could see the color rising in her cheeks.

"No problem."

And he slipped off into the night.

***

Clara closed the door behind Aaron, wondering what had possessed her to kiss him. She reset the alarm and crawled into bed. With no one else around, Clara let her thoughts willingly wander to Aaron as she drifted off to sleep.

CHAPTER THREE

Aleksandr was home the next day, and that night he came into the bedroom where Clara was reading in bed.

"I just had the security company fax me over a copy of the latest activity," he said.

"Mmm." She was only half listening.

"It shows that last night the alarm was set at 9:25," he said, looking at the paper in his hand. "Then disarmed at 10:36, and re-armed at 11:01."

Shit. That security company.

Clara ran scenarios as quickly as she could through her head. She couldn't use Ryan because Aleksandr would clearly verify with him.

"I had set the alarm," she explained, "but then decided to go out on the balcony awhile longer since I couldn't sleep. I had a glass of wine. I think I may have even left the glass out there." She knew Ryan would never volunteer that he had enjoyed a glass of wine with the boss's wife, and since she had already washed and put his glass away, there was nothing to suggest he had.

"Yes," said Aleksandr, frowning. "I found it when I got home."

Clara kicked off the covers. It was time for damage control. She kneeled on the foot of the bed where he was still standing, and placed her hands on his rigid chest.

"I'm sorry, dear," she said. "It won't happen again."

Aleksandr took her face with both hands and kissed her, and Clara tried to go to her happy place. To try and remember that she had once been in love with this man, had craved his touch before she knew what a monster he was.

His hands slid down her throat and pushed the straps of her slip off her shoulders, making Clara's skin crawl. But she knew reacting would only make it worse.

Aleksandr's phone rang and Clara gave a silent prayer. He pulled away, the cleft in his chin more pronounced by his frown, and answered it in Ukrainian.

Whatever it was, it clearly wasn't good. He hung up and grabbed his blazer from the chair.

"I have to go," he growled. "Don't wait up."

"Okay," she said.

The alarm beeped, indicating that Aleksandr had set it as he left. She was unchaperoned at the moment, but now that she knew her husband was monitoring the security system, she was still a prisoner in her own house.

She grabbed her cell and called Aaron. This time it went to voicemail.

"Hey," she said. "I just wanted to make sure you got out of here all right last night. If he's looked at the video, he didn't find anything. However, it turns out he's been keeping tabs on the alarm system, so even though I'm here alone," she sighed, "I still can't go anywhere. Anyway, call me back and let me know you're okay." She hung up and waited for the phone to ring. And waited. And waited.

***

Aaron listened to the message and immediately deleted it. What the hell was Clara thinking? If Morozov was monitoring the security system, who's to say he wasn't going over her phone statement with a fine-toothed comb? Even if she was deleting the call history, it would still show up on a printout.

And she was calling just to say hi. To check in with him. Hadn't he told her they needed to lay low?

But a small part of him was glad she had called, had enjoyed hearing her voice again, and had been relieved to know that she was safe.

Aaron picked up a pen off the counter and flung it across the room.

Dammit! I won't let a woman fuck things up for me like it did for Reid.

It was time to get his head on straight before his personal feeling got in the way of his career.

He sent an encrypted message asking Gavin to meet him, then walked to the nearby café to wait.

***

Aaron was on his second cup of coffee when Gavin walked in.

"Took you long enough," he said as Gavin sat down.

"You're not my only case, you know," said Gavin. "Now what's up?"

"I think you need to take me off this assignment."

"Why? Have you been compromised?"

Yes. "No," Aaron answered. "Just not sure I'm the best man for the job anymore."

Gavin closed his eyes and massaged the bridge of his nose. "I feel a headache coming on," he said. "And who exactly do you feel *is* the best man for the job?"

"I don't know. But it's not me."

"What's going on?" asked Gavin. "What are you not telling me?"

"Nothing. It just feels like I've hit a dead end.

[38]

Morozov moved everything out of his home office and now Clara doesn't know how she'll get access to anything. Plus his phone calls are giving us shit. The guy's too careful."

"Then what do you propose we do?" said Gavin. "Close up shop and call it a loss?"

Aaron remembered Clara begging him to let her help put Morozov away. She was stuck in a living hell and the only escape was taking him down.

"No," he said, "that's not what I mean. But maybe a fresh pair of eyes will help."

"Listen, Wells, if you can give one good reason why you shouldn't be on this case, just one, then I will be more than happy to pull you off. But Clara Morozov trusts you, and you two have established a protocol. Let's not mess that up if we don't have to."

Aaron sighed. "Fine." Like it or not, he really w*as* the best man for the job. He just needed to work harder at not letting his attraction for Aleksandr Morozov's wife get in his way.

***

The next morning Clara woke relieved that her husband had already left for the morning, but irritated that Aaron had never returned her call. Worry entered her mind, but she couldn't imagine what trouble he may have found, so it was quickly replaced with more irritation.

She had pretended to be asleep when Aleksandr

made it home around two a.m. and thought he might want to continue where they had left off, but he had simply crawled into bed and was snoring shortly after.

She showered and walked down to the main level, where Ryan was sitting on the couch waiting for her to start her day.

"Good morning, Mrs. Morozov. What shall we do today?" he asked.

Clara walked into the kitchen, poured a cup of coffee, and leaned against the counter, wondering, what *should* she do today.

"You know what, Ryan?" she said. "Let's go to the restaurant today for lunch."

"The restaurant, ma'am? You mean your husband's restaurant?"

His hesitation didn't surprise her. The Morozov woman usually avoided the place except for family events. It was more of a boys' club, really.

"Of course. Is that a problem?" she asked.

"Um, no, ma'am. No problem. Let me know when you're ready to go."

***

Clara walked into Dimitre's wearing leggings, an off-the-shoulder sweater, and a pair of simple pumps. Flattering enough that the boys would be happy to see her, but not revealing enough to piss off her husband.

And it worked, because all eyes were upon her as soon as she stepped into the backroom. All six men stood, including a stranger she had never met before, but only Aleksandr walked over to kiss her cheek.

"Clara, what a...surprise," he said. "What are you doing here?"

She tried to pick up any irritation in his voice, but if it was there, he was doing a good job at hiding it.

"I just thought I would come have lunch with you. After you surprised me with dinner last week, I thought I would return the favor."

Her husband looked at her with skepticism. "And so you decided to come *here* for lunch?"

"Leave her alone," one of the cousins, Yurik, said. "We haven't seen Clara in forever. Stephan," he called out, "go grab another chair so she can sit with us for a minute."

But the stranger stepped back from his seat and spoke in a charming British accent. "She may have mine. I was just about to head out."

Clara walked over, and he held out a hand that she accepted.

"You must be Aleksandr's beautiful wife, Clara," he said, and she nodded before giving a nervous glance towards her husband.

"This is Tristan Brandt," Aleksandr explained. "He owns the gallery where we will be attending the fundraiser this weekend."

[41]

"I see," she said. "Well, it's a pleasure to meet you."

"Your husband is interested in purchasing some new artwork for the restaurant, so I thought I would stop by and get a feel for the atmosphere before suggesting any pieces."

Clara looked right into his smiling blue eyes and knew that he was lying. But what did she care? "Can't wait to see what we end up with," she said dryly.

"I hope we have a chance to chat more this weekend," he said, releasing her hand, "but if you'll excuse me, I have other matters to attend to." He turned to the rest of the table. "Gentlemen."

They all nodded their goodbyes and sat down along with Clara.

"So how are you, Clara?" Yurik asked her.

"I'm doing much better," she said. "I apologize that I haven't been very good company lately. Not since…the accident."

They all nodded somberly, except for Aleksandr, who was still watching her with scrutiny, and she avoided his eye.

"It's good to see you looking well again," said Stephan on her right as he patted her hand.

"Stephan here was just telling us that my sister is pregnant with their third child," Aleksandr announced. Four heads head snapped in his direction, then back to Clara, but no one said anything, including Clara, who again bit her tongue as the anger boiled up inside.

Everyone seemed to be holding their breath, until she turned to Stephen and gave him her best smile. "Congratulations, Stephan. I'm very excited for you two."

Stephan gave an awkward grin.

"Perhaps we should move out to the dining room for a more intimate lunch, Clara my dear," said Aleksandr.

Clara would have much preferred to stay seated at that table with all of them, but she knew they weren't going to let anything slip with her sitting among them.

"Of course."

They all stood again with Clara, and she and her husband chose one of the more private booths in the dining room. The restaurant was rarely crowded, so it wasn't difficult to find a place.

"What are you playing at?" he asked, filling their wine glasses from a bottle he had grabbed on the way out.

"Nothing," she said. "I was feeling nostalgic for the old days, and I really did want to surprise you. Is it so wrong to want to spend time with you?"

"Oh, that's rich," he laughed. "Because I'm pretty sure all you've been trying to do lately is get away from me." Aleksandr swirled his wine glass and looked her right in the eye.

How many times had Clara cowered under that glare? But not today.

"I'm trying to make an effort," she lied. "I'm trying to be a better wife." She reached across the table and took his hand. "Can't we try to make a fresh start?"

Aleksandr squeezed her hand back. Hard. With his other hand he took a slow sip of his wine, all the while tightening the grip on her hand. Clara did her best not to grimace or pull her hand free.

"Hmm…" he said, finally releasing her. "We shall see."

***

Aleksandr pushed his plate back and looked at his watch.

"I need to get back to business," he said.

Clara emptied the wine bottle into her glass. "I'll just finish this off and then I should head out as well."

He slid out of the booth then leaned over his wife to kiss her goodbye.

"Will you be home tonight?" she asked. "Maybe I could make something special for dinner."

"I'm afraid I'll be late again." He put his lips to her ear. "But perhaps you could make something special for dessert."

Her eyes closed and she tried to maintain her

[44]

composure.

"Of course," she said, opening them and forcing a smile. "Anything for my husband."

Aleksandr sneered at her as he walked away.

Clara polished off the wine glass in one gulp. She cleared the plates and got to work on the real reason she had come here. When the coast was clear, she sneaked into the storage closet and closed the door behind her.

Back when she had worked here as a server, Clara had accidentally discovered that voices from the back room carried through the vent in here. Not well, but perhaps if she put her ear to it, she might pick up something useful.

Most of it she couldn't make out, but Yurik's voice, being the biggest, came through clear enough.

"Tell me again, how many girls this time?" he said.

Clara couldn't make out the response, but she assumed he was referring to prostitutes. Thank God Bobbi's husband, Stephan, had never really mastered Ukrainian, forcing this conversation to be in English.

"And a grand a piece is the agreed upon price?" said Yurik.

She thought those were some expensive hookers, but what did she know?

"Nice, very nice indeed. Stephan, you have all buyers confirmed?"

Buyers? Was Aleksandr in the pimp business now?

[45]

It didn't make sense to her, but nothing about her husband really surprised her anymore.

Somebody turned the handle of the closet, and Clara tried to get off the floor as quickly as possible. She was still on one knee when one of the busboys came in.

"Hey, I was just trying to find more disinfectant for wiping the tables down," she said.

Confusion was all over the kid's face. "Who are you?" he asked.

She stood the rest of the way up, dusted off her pants, and put a hand on her hip. "I'm Clara Morozov. Aleksandr Morozov's wife."

The confusion was replaced with surprise. "Oh! It's right here." He grabbed a jug from behind her.

"Good," she said. "Now I want you to dump all the buckets and put fresh solution in them before you wipe any more tables. I hate seeing tables wiped down with dirty water."

"Of course, Mrs. Morozov. I'll get right on that Mrs. Morozov." And he rushed out with the bottle.

Clara grabbed her purse and left just as quickly.

***

"How was your lunch, Mrs. Morozov?" Ryan asked from the front seat as they drove across the I-90 Bridge back into Bellevue.

"It was good, really good," she said. She had managed to get more info, which was a plus, but she

[46]

wasn't sure what to make of it. Was the Morozov family getting into prostitution? And did it have anything to do with the container that was arriving from China in only two weeks? But what would a shipping container have to do with a bunch of girls?

And then Clara's heart stopped as she put it all together.

Oh God, my husband is trafficking girls! She had to tell Aaron.

"Ryan, could we swing by the library?" she asked as calmly as possible. "There's a book I want to look for."

"Of course, Mrs. Morozov."

CHAPTER FOUR

Aaron was sitting at his computer trying to weed out all the obviously legitimate containers on the ship from Hong Kong. So far he had whittled the list down to two hundred thirty-six. Still not great, but better than five hundred.

The phone rang and he let it go to voicemail again, as was procedure. Hopefully Clara had something better to say other than 'how are you.'

He listened to the message.

"I have information for you," she said. "I think I've figured it out. I'm at the library, meet me as soon as you can."

"This had better be good," Aaron muttered as he grabbed his jacket.

***

Aaron jogged up to the second level and found

Clara by the books with her back to him. The sight of her stole his breath as he took in her long, slender legs and the way the heels shaped her calves. Her thick copper hair was twisted in a knot, exposing her neck and a shoulder where the sweater hung off it. He fought the urge to run his tongue across the smooth, pale skin.

He must have been thinking too hard, because she turned around and blushed.

"You have something," he said, ignoring her reaction.

"Yes." She pulled him to a more private corner before continuing. "I don't have much time, but I think I know what's in the container, and it's not guns or drugs."

"What else could it be?" he asked, furrowing his brow.

"Girls. Human girls. He already has buyers for them and is selling them for a thousand each."

"Human trafficking? Are you sure?"

She nodded. "I was able to eavesdrop on them at the restaurant today."

"Do you know how many?"

Her head shook. "I was only able to hear part of the conversation."

Aaron rubbed his chin. "He must have an inside man then."

"What do you mean?" she asked.

"If it was just guns or drugs he was smuggling, that would be easy to hide in artifacts, to cover them up until you get past customs. But you can't slip a box full of living people past border inspections. You need to know someone." His face lit up. "This is it, this the break we needed!"

"Really?"

"Yes," said Aaron. "We need to focus on the agents. Something is sure to turn up for whoever is dirty." He grabbed her with the biggest smile on his face and kissed her cheek. "You're brilliant, Clara!"

The color rushed to her cheeks again and she smiled.

"All you need to do now is sit tight. I can take the rest from here."

"Okay."

***

Clara and Aleksandr sat in the back seat as Ryan drove them to a fundraiser in Seattle. Even though it had been two days since she had heard from Aaron, she felt a weight had been lifted off her shoulders. No more secrecy, no more fear of being caught. All that was left now was to sit back and wait for Aaron and his men to take her husband down.

Then sweet freedom. Clara took a deep, contented breath, already smelling it.

But she'd forgotten whose company she was in.

Aleksandr gave her hand a gentle squeeze.

"You look exquisite, my dear."

She smiled and adjusted his bow tie. "You don't look so bad yourself," she said. "Seeing you in a tux always reminds me of our wedding day."

Aleksandr looked pleased, but it only brought the familiar heartache for Clara.

***

The event was just as Clara had expected. A lot of boring, pretentious people schmoozing each other, and her husband pretending to be an upstanding, charitable citizen of the community.

From a corner drinking her champagne, she surveyed the crowd and scoffed at the hilarity of it all. While Aleksandr had managed to insert himself into this crowd, something his father had never been able to succeed at, Clara knew it was only because of all the dirt he had on them. Would they pretend to be shocked when he was finally arrested, she wondered. She smiled as she imagined the headlines.

"I don't know why everyone is so eager to come to these things," a nearby guest said as she tugged uncomfortably at her dress. "I always find them to be so stuffy."

"I couldn't agree with you more," said Clara, and she clinked glasses with the blonde before taking another sip. Her gaze fell upon the woman's diamond pendant necklace.

"That's a beautiful piece," Clara said, nodding

[51]

towards her throat.

"Why, thank you," she said, touching it. "It was my grandmother's. I'm Sydney, by the way. Sydney Holden."

Sydney held out her hand and Clara shook it.

"Clara Morozov."

"Morozov?" Sydney asked. "Any relation to Aleksandr Morozov?"

"He's my husband. Do you know him?

"I just met him tonight. My fiancé owns this gallery. Tristan Brandt?"

"I've met him," Clara said with a little less warmth in her words. "I hear he's helping my husband with some artwork." She narrowed her eyes, waiting for Sydney's reaction.

"You'll be happy," she said with a big grin on her face. "Tristan really has an eye."

Clara wondered if Sydney was really that naive. But hadn't she been when she and Aleksandr met all those years ago?

"How long have you two been together?" Clara asked.

"A little over two years. He only just popped the question last week," Sydney gushed, and then leaned in closer. "Between you and me, I was beginning to think it would never happen."

"Congratulations," Clara said. If Sydney was lucky, Tristan would leave her before they ever walked down the aisle.

"I think I'm being summoned," Sydney said with a sigh. "My face is staring to hurt from all the smiling."

"I know how that goes."

Clara watched her weave through the crowd to Brandt. Sydney pointed in her direction and Tristan raised a glass, giving her a sly smile.

"You smug son of a bitch," she muttered, raising her glass in return.

"Good Evening, Mrs. Morozov."

Clara turned to see yet another guest had appeared at her side.

"Might I say you look radiant tonight?" he said.

"Evening, Senator Jameson."

"Please, call me Paul." He flashed one of his trademark megawatt smiles.

"Very well, then, Paul. How are you?"

"Better for having set my gaze upon your magnificent form!" he said with a slight slur to his words.

She laughed politely. "I see you've been enjoying the open bar."

"I hear your husband has been spending a lot of time on business trips lately."

"Have you now?" she asked with a raised eyebrow.

The senator leaned in close to her ear while brushing his knuckles against her bare arm, and she tasted a little bile in the back of her throat.

"If there's ever anything I can do for you," he whispered, "*anything* at all. Don't ever be afraid to ask."

He pulled back with a sickening smile on his face. And there was Aleksandr right behind him.

She had done nothing wrong, but his glare said it all. She would pay.

She tried to keep her voice from trembling as she spoke.

"Senator Jameson, you know my husband," she said, keeping eye contact with her husband.

Jameson turned around and shook Aleksandr's hand as though he hadn't just tried to solicit the man's wife.

"Aleksandr, my boy, how are you?" said the senator.

"I'm well," Aleksandr answered dryly, still holding her gaze. "And yourself?"

"Good, good," he said, giving a little cough. "I was just telling your lovely wife here that if you kids need anything, you know how to reach me."

With a stone face, Aleksandr looked Jameson in the eye. "Were you now?"

Clara could almost hear the click as Jameson realized he had just hit on the wrong man's wife.

"I—I…" he stuttered.

Aleksandr reached out for Clara's hand and she reluctantly took it. "If you'll excuse us, senator," he

[54]

said. "I think it's time I took my wife home. I'm afraid she has enjoyed a bit too much champagne."

Her other hand shook as she placed her glass on a nearby table, almost spilling it. No words were exchanged as he led her to the entrance, where they waited for the car to be brought around. But on the inside, Clara was screaming for someone to save her.

***

The rain pounding on the car's roof was the only sound as they drove back into Bellevue until Clara couldn't stand it anymore.

"The senator approached me!" she said. "What was I supposed to do? Slap him right there in front of everybody? You're the one always reminding me not to make a fool of myself in front of people."

Aleksandr's jaw remained tight, eyes forward.

"This is not my fault," she said. Tears were threatening to fall. "Not my fault," she whispered.

He finally turned to her. "You're the one who wore that dress. Of course Jameson would approach you."

"You chose it for me," she said, raising her voice.

"I should have known better. The man always had a weakness for whores."

Maybe she really did have too much champagne because she slapped him without even thinking about it.

Aleksandr calmly touched his cheek where she had struck him, and her hands flew to her face.

"I'm so sorry," she said, "I—" But the back of Aleksandr's hand cut her off. And then it flew at her again. This time Clara blocked the assault, pissing him off that much more. He quickly released his seat belt, shoving her against the passenger door, trying to get his hands around her throat. She clawed at his face, fighting him off as best she could.

"Ryan, stop the car!" It was a half cry, half scream. And it was pointless. She knew no one would dare save her from her husband. "Please," she yelled, trying to push Aleksandr off of her.

"Yes, Ryan, stop the car!" he suddenly shouted.

Clara was dumbstruck as Ryan immediately followed his orders.

Aleksandr reached for the door handle and pushed Clara onto the pavement as it opened.

"Get out, you bitch!" he yelled, and then ordered Ryan to drive as he closed it again.

The car drove away, leaving Clara heaped in a gutter as the rain continued to pour down on her. There was no traffic on the side street, and Clara was glad there hadn't been a witness to the unceremonious dump. She stood and picked up a shoe that had come off. The other one must have come off in the car where it remained. Along with her purse and cell phone. She started limping along the sidewalk, not knowing where she was going. When she got to the next intersection, she realized she was within walking distance to Aaron's building. It was the last place she should be right now. But it was the only place she thought she might be safe.

***

As Aaron approached the door to the building carrying a grocery bag, he thought he was seeing things. Because standing in front of it was the last person he'd expect to see here.

"What are you doing here?" he asked Clara, who had the nerve to look relieved to see him.

"I'm sorry," she said. "I didn't know where else to go."

He took stock of her and realized she was soaked from head to toe with a single shoe in her left hand. Her wet hair was matted against her face, almost hiding a fresh bruise on her cheek.

Aaron cupped her face to take a better look. "Jesus Christ. Did he do this to you?"

She could only nod.

His head was spinning and he had to take a step back.

"Why are you here, Clara?" he asked. "Does Aleksandr know you're here?"

"No," she shook her head, "I don't think so."

"You don't think so," he said, raising his voice more than he'd intended. "What do you mean, *you don't think so?*"

Clara's chin trembled; she looked ready to crumble.

[57]

"He pushed me out of the car and drove off. He left me without any money or a phone. I have nothing." A sob caught in her throat and she took a deep breath before continuing. "I told you, I didn't know where else to go. As far as I know I wasn't followed."

Aaron didn't blame her for showing up at his door. In light of the events, it was probably the best move. It wouldn't have been smart to go to the police, and really, what could they do for her? She sure as hell couldn't go back to Aleksandr.

What kind of man beats his wife and then dumps her on the street?

The problem was he didn't know if he could trust himself with Clara, sweet vulnerable Clara, here, in such a confined space with him.

"Let's get you upstairs," he said, ignoring his concerns. "We'll get you cleaned up."

"Thank you," she whispered.

She followed him up to his apartment. He dropped the bag on the counter and stepped into the bathroom, pulled a towel off the bar, and walked to where Clara was still standing by the door.

"You know this complicates things," he said, wrapping the towel around her shoulders. "You being here."

"I know."

And before he knew what was happening, Clara was on her toes, pressing her mouth against his.

Aaron pushed her back, keeping a firm grip on her shoulders, and she let the shoe drop to the floor.

"I shouldn't have done that," she said, touching her luscious pink lips.

It surprised Aaron just as much as her when he pulled her back into him and kissed her, this time slipping his tongue past her lips.

She started it, he tried to tell himself as his tongue explored her mouth and tasted how sweet she was. It reminded him of bubbles. Of champagne.

One step forward and her back was now against the door. The same door that Aaron knew he should be marching her out of, but now he had no intention of letting her walk through it anytime soon.

***

Aaron took a breath and pressed his forehead against hers. "This is wrong, Clara. So wrong."

Clara's heart was pounding, and her breasts heaved in quick succession against him. "Then maybe you should ask me to leave," she said.

"I think we both know that's not going to happen."

She kissed him with an urgency she never thought she would feel for anyone ever again.

She felt his hand on her waist, groping for the top of a zipper, while Clara ran her hands through Aaron's short, dark hair. It was softer than she had expected. Even his touch was gentle as he slowly pulled the zipper down. Their mouths remained pressed together as he pulled her arms down to push the dress off, leaving her with only the black underwear and strapless bra.

When her arms were free again she immediately tugged at the hem of his shirt, and they had to part lips so she could get it off him. He leaned back into her and the hot flesh burned into Clara's still cold, wet skin. She wanted to be on fire with this man.

Aaron's tongue traced a line down her neck and back up to her ear, where he sucked and bit at it, causing her to moan. She wrapped her right leg around him, and he cupped her thigh, grinding his pelvis against hers. Clara couldn't remember the last time she wanted someone this badly and was going to explode if he wasn't inside her soon.

He must have been reading her desires, because Aaron grabbed the other thigh, and with her arms around his neck, hoisted her off the floor and carried her the few short paces to his queen-size bed in a corner of the tiny studio apartment. He kneeled on the bed with her still hanging onto him and carefully laid her back on the pillow. Clara wanted to cry from the softness of it all. He leaned over to kiss her, and as her chest lifted off the bed to press against his, he reached underneath and made quick work of the bra. His tongue again traced a path down to a rosy erect nipple, and she gave a little moan as his tongue flicked across it. His right hand began massaging it while his mouth moved to the opposite breast to give it equal attention. Clara was in sweet agony. She wanted release, but the torture felt so good, she wasn't sure she ever wanted it to end.

Aaron came back up to kiss her lips, and his right hand worked its way down her body, slipped beneath the now wet satin to tease her even more. God, she was so close. If he just moved his thumb up a little…. But his hand disappeared altogether and pushed the last remaining clothing down her legs. He sat up to get them off completely before laying on top of her again, still clothed in his jeans. Clara's hands reached down to unbutton them and then struggled to push them down. She managed to get them low enough to free his bulge, and it was enough for her. She needed him now. But Aaron slid off the bed and pulled them off completely.

He was so beautiful. His broad shoulders, muscular legs, and rock solid abs reminded her of a Spartan warrior. Even his skin was darker than she had imagined.

He carefully climbed back up, kissing her before slowly sliding into her. Clara's fingers dug into his skin as she threw her head back in ecstasy, thrusting her hips into him. She felt so full. No, not full. She felt whole. As though Aaron were literally her missing piece.

"Oh, Clara," he moaned into her ear. "My sweet

Clara."

The beauty of it all was too much for her, and tears started to fill her eyes. But she didn't want Aaron to see—she didn't want him to worry, or worse yet, panic, so she buried her face into his chest as he continued to move in and out of her. His scent surrounded her, the heady mix of musk and perspiration, and it was enough to do her in. A fire that started in her belly spread throughout her entire body. They continued to move together, and Clara relished every second of it. The feel of his lips against her skin, his hand sliding along her body. It wasn't long before another wave swept through her body, and she felt Aaron tense against her hands and knew he was coming with her.

***

Aaron lay next to Clara as she remained on her back, trying to catch her breath. He ran a hand down her side and took pleasure in watching her whole body quiver under his touch.

Turning on her side to face him, he saw a smile on her face that had to match his own, and he couldn't help but kiss it.

"What now?" she asked, and Aaron's smile faltered.

"What do you mean?" he said.

She propped her head up in her hand. "Well, as much as I would like to stay here with you for the rest of the night..."she trailed off.

Aaron kissed her and pushed her back onto the pillow. "We just had the most incredible sex, and you're ready to leave me already."

"Mmm....It was pretty amazing, wasn't it?" she said with a smile.

"But as much as I hate to admit it," he said, "you're right. It probably wouldn't be smart for you to spend the night here." He frowned as he caressed her cheek. "However, I don't feel comfortable sending you back to the asshole who did this to you either."

Being this close, Aaron could see the little flecks of gold around the pupil in her otherwise bright green eyes.

"What other options do we have?" she asked.

The frown remained, but he gave a sigh. "Fine." He slid out of bed. "Can I at least dry your dress for you before you go back out there?"

"Oh no," she said. "It's couture. You don't just throw something like that into the dryer. Not that it isn't already ruined beyond repair," she muttered.

"Couture," he said, sitting on the bed next to her. "I don't even know what that means."

She sat up and kissed his shoulder with a smile. "Basically that's a fancy way of saying a very expensive dress."

"Must be nice to have so much money you get to buy dresses that have fancy words for saying they're really expensive."

Clara's face went dark and he immediately regretted the words.

"Oh, I pay dearly for them," she said in a hushed tone. "And I would gladly give them all up."

***

"I don't understand how you ended up with Aleksandr Morozov in the first place," he said, turning to face her better. He was finally asking the questions that had been burning inside of him. "All of our intel has told us that everyone in that family is Ukrainian, even the spouses. The family doesn't care much for outsiders."

"Oh, yes. Many of them don't care much for me, mainly my mother-in-law. But Aleksandr always did things his own way. And as the third son, no one ever expected him to take over the family business. So while they weren't happy about our engagement, in the end, his father decided it didn't really matter."

"But how did you two even meet?" Aaron asked. "How does an Irish foster girl end up marrying into a Ukrainian mafia family?"

"I didn't know they were the mafia," she said. "I didn't really believe they existed anymore. And even in the movies they were usually Italian."

Aaron waited patiently for her to continue.

"We met at the restaurant," she explained. "Aleksandr's father, Dimitre, knew that the best legitimate business front was one with real customers and everything. It was staffed mostly by family members, but he hired a few outsiders to make it look that much more legit. I started working there my senior year in high school, trying to save money for college."

"And you had no idea what kind of person he was?"

"Do you think I would have married him if I had?" she asked, frowning at him. But then her expression softened as she focused on something over his shoulder. "He was different then. Not fully developed, you might say. There were signs, I now realize, but I misread them. A patron once grabbed my ass as I walked by and Aleksandr broke his nose." She sighed. "I thought he was my knight in shining armor. No one could hurt me as long as he was around. Little did I know he was the one I needed protecting from.

"It wasn't until after we were married," she continued, "that I began to see what he was really capable of. Then when his father and older brothers were killed by the car bomb and Aleksandr took over, well that's when I saw him in all his glory."

"Why didn't you leave?" Aaron asked softly.

She laughed, but it was cold. "You don't think I tried?"

There was a long pause as Clara looked down at

her hands. Aaron reached out and took one of them.

"I still dreamed of college," she said. "But he said there was no need now that I had him to take care of me. We argued about it until he slammed me against a wall and told me I would do well to remember my place in this house.

"Shortly after that, I asked for a divorce." She finally met his eye. "Let's just say that didn't go well. Morozovs don't get divorced. Ever. The first time I got the courage to walk out, he dragged me from the car by my hair."

Aaron was trying to remain calm. None of this was a surprise for him. He'd had his suspicions after seeing the bruise under her scarf. To hear her say it, though, in her own words….Aaron wouldn't have thought it possible to hate Morozov more than he had before taking on this mission.

"What about friends or family?" he asked. "Or even the police?" But he was sure he knew the answer.

"What family? After my parents died, I was bounced around so many foster families and group homes. And what few friends I did have were lost by the time I married Aleksandr. I was the perfect victim. Nobody would miss me if I disappeared."

Aaron frowned.

"As for police," she continued, "I had no way of knowing which ones were in his pocket. It was too risky."

"But you tried again, didn't you? You said, 'the first time.' That means there was another time."

Clara looked away again, and the expression on her face made his heart ache. Could the story really get worse?

"When we found out we were expecting," she started, and Aaron gasped. "Aleksandr was over the moon about it. Now that he was head of the family, a child, an heir, was something he wanted desperately. I noticed that his anger had lessened, he was more gentle with me. I thought it was my chance to escape unharmed. To save us both."

Aaron shook his head and she kept talking.

"I ended up in the ER that night."

"You lost the baby, didn't you?" he whispered.

She closed her eyes and nodded, a single tear trailing down her cheek. He wiped it away and she opened her eyes again.

"Not only did I lose the baby," she said, "but the damage was so severe that I will never be able to carry another child."

"What did Morozov say when he found out?"

"He doesn't know."

"What do you mean he doesn't know?" Aaron asked.

"I was able to convince the doctor not to tell him. Because when he does find out, I become useless to him. I would be…removed, and he would find a proper Ukrainian wife. One that can bear him an heir to his empire." She took both of Aaron's hands and squeezed them tight, looking into his eyes. "Do you understand now why I need him to be taken down? I'm living on borrowed time until he figures it out."

"How long ago did this happen? When you lost the baby, I mean."

"Four months ago."

***

Aaron grabbed his phone and started dialing.

"What are you doing?" she asked.

"I'm arranging protection for you. You can't stay here, obviously, but I'll be damned if you're going back to Morozov."

Clara sat on the bed still wrapped up in his sheets without saying a word while he sent the encrypted message for Gavin to meet him at the diner again. He grabbed his jacket and sat down next to her.

"You'll be safe here. I won't be gone long, and then they will probably want to get you to a safehouse right away."

She nodded and then pulled his face into hers, where he kissed her long and slow.

"Be careful," she whispered.

***

"Twice in one week, Wells," Gavin said as he sat down. "Is it my birthday or something?"

"We need to pull Clara Morozov out," said Aaron. "Get her to a safehouse."

Gavin rolled his eyes. "And why would we do that?"

"Because she's not safe in Aleksandr's custody."

"What do you mean, custody? She's his god-damned wife."

"Only because he won't let her leave. Her life is in danger every second she's with him."

"That's not our problem. Our mission was to gather intel to take Morozov down. His wife approached us and offered her services, not the other way around."

"So what are you saying?"

"I'm saying we can't risk the operation. We are *this* close to taking down the head of one of the biggest Ukrainian crime syndicates on the West Coast. It may even lead to more busts. If we pull Clara Morozov out now, he may get spooked and this will all be for nothing."

"He could kill her any day now," Aaron said, slamming his fist on the table.

"You don't know that," said Gavin.

"But what if he does? Do we just chalk that up to collateral damage?"

"What the hell has gotten into you?"

"I just—" But Aaron wasn't sure how to answer without betraying himself.

"Have you developed feelings for this woman?" Gavin asked. "Oh my God." He leaned in, whispering the rest. "Did you fucking sleep with Aleksandr Morozov's wife?"

"What? No!" But Aaron knew Gavin didn't buy it for a second.

"Shit," Gavin muttered, burying his face in his hands.

"I didn't—She—" But again, there was nothing Aaron could say to help his case.

Gavin lifted his head. "Listen, for the sake of both our careers, we're going to pretend this didn't happen. Clara Morozov stays with Aleksandr and plays nice little wifey to her husband until we're able to make the raid. Do you understand?"

Aaron frowned and tried to think up an argument.

"Do you understand, Agent Wells?" Gavin repeated.

"Yes, sir."

"Good. And try and keep your dick in your pants from now on." Gavin stood up, tossed down a couple ones, and walked out.

Aaron sat there a few minutes longer, wondering how he was going to tell Clara that she was going to have to go home to the man she feared most.

CHAPTER FIVE

Clara was sitting on Aaron's bed when he walked in the door, but now she was wearing one of his t-shirts. The hopeful expression in her eyes made him sick to his stomach.

"What's the plan?" she asked.

He sat next to her and took her hand in his. His mouth just couldn't form the words he needed to tell her.

"They need me to go back to Aleksandr, don't they?" she said.

"I'm sorry."

"He'll get suspicious if I don't come back."

Aaron nodded.

"I'll get dressed," she said, standing up. "If you'll drop me off somewhere nearby, I'll call him from there."

Aaron got up and followed her to the front door, where her dress was still lying in a heap. "How can you be so calm about this? After what he just did to you? Have you not seen the bruise on your cheek?"

Clara's hand went up to where Morozov had hit her earlier. She picked up the still-wet garment and struggled to put it on.

"Because it's what needs to be done," she said. "And this is the least of what he has done to me."

Aaron's stomach turned.

"Will you help me with this?" she asked.

But instead of helping, Aaron stopped her by grabbing both hands. "Let's run away. Right now. I have assets I could liquidate, not to mention other resources. I can have papers made tonight and we'll disappear together."

Aaron couldn't believe what he was saying. After all the grief he gave Reid Jackson for leaving the agency over a girl and now here he was talking about not only leaving the agency, but going AWOL. And he was dead serious. If going on the run was what he needed to do to keep Clara safe, he wasn't going to hesitate.

But she shook her head. "Running away won't change anything."

"Of course it would," he said. "It would get you away from Aleksandr. He would never be able to hit you again."

"No, it wouldn't. Don't you understand? He would never let this go. I can't spend the rest of my life looking over my shoulder wondering if he's going to find me. Haven't I spent enough of my life living in fear?"

Aaron stared into her green eyes, struggling for an argument against what she was saying, but Clara was right. She would never be truly safe until Morozov was behind bars, or even better yet, dead.

"If you really want to help me," said Clara, "take him down. Make sure there are no mistakes, that there is no way he can get off."

"I promise," he said and reluctantly helped her back into the dress, cherishing every moment his hand made contact with her warm skin.

"Are you ready?" he asked.

He saw the fear in her eyes, but Clara just stuck out her chin and nodded. She was, without a doubt, the strongest woman he knew.

***

Aaron dropped Clara off a block from the nearest gas station and she wanted to cry. She had no idea what was in store for her once Aleksandr came for her. But she looked over at Aaron and knew what she was leaving behind—a man who would never raise his hand to her, who wanted to protect her, who only ten minutes ago had offered to give up everything to run away with her, and a man who, Clara realized, she was in love with.

"It's not too late," Aaron said, as if reading her thoughts. "We could still run away. They might be able to pull this off with you gone."

She shook her head.

"I know," he said and took her hand. "Promise you'll call me at the first sign of trouble. I'd rather be on the run with you than lose you."

She lost it at his words.

"Oh Clara." Aaron reached across the seat and pulled her into his arms.

For a moment she let herself cry into his chest, feeling the warmth of his body and breathing in his masculine scent. But then it was time to pull herself together. Even just sitting in this car wrapped up in his arms was dangerous. What if someone saw them? She reluctantly pulled away and he let her go.

The word goodbye felt incredibly inappropriate in this moment, so she simply opened her door and got out. It didn't surprise her that he didn't drive away until she was at the door.

She took a deep breath to steady herself, walked in, and stepped up to the counter. "I need to borrow your phone, please."

***

Aaron watched Clara walk inside before forcing himself to drive away. He tried telling himself that he was doing the right thing, letting her go in alone. But it didn't feel right.

As he drove back to the apartment, Aaron wondered how he had gotten himself into this mess. He was starting to think maybe he owed Reid an apology.

***

Clara stood outside the gas station, waiting. She assumed Aleksandr was coming to get her, but she couldn't be sure from the crisp conversation.

"Where are you?" he had asked upon answering the phone.

"The Chevron on Main."

Click.

The town car pulled up and Ryan jumped out to open the passenger door. She was relieved to see the backseat was empty. There was pity in Ryan's eyes, and Clara found herself pitying him as well. For all the times her husband had hit her, for all the fresh bruises everyone had pretended not to notice, this was the first time there had been witnesses. But it didn't really change anything. No one would dare go against Aleksandr.

Except Aaron, she reminded herself. *He will save me.* It was a ray of hope that Clara needed to hold on to if she was going to get through the next few days.

No one said anything for the short drive home. What could they say to each other?

Aleksandr was nowhere to be found when she

walked in. and at first she was thankful for his absence, but the gratitude quickly turned to anxiety. The storm was still coming, it was just a matter of when, and the suspense was putting her on edge.

She made her way to the master bath, turned on the shower, and for the second time that evening, slipped out of the wet dress and kicked it into a corner. It was completely ruined.

The hot water ran over her body, and for the first time she took notice of the scrapes along her hands and back of her thighs where she had hit the pavement. How had she not seen these before? And then she blushed as she remembered where her attention had been focused at the time. Just then the door to the bathroom opened and she held her breath. He was home.

***

She turned the water off and quickly reached for the towel, but Aleksandr beat her to it. Instead of handing it to her, he leaned against the bathroom counter and looked over her naked body. Clara was sure that her infidelity was etched into her skin, and for a brief moment, she regretted being with Aaron. But then he gave the towel to her and she wrapped it around herself.

"Where were you?" he asked.

"What does it matter?" she said.

"Really? You ready to go for round two?"

The anger was written all over Aleksandr's face, but instead of being afraid, Clara found herself filling with rage. She wanted nothing more than to go at him with everything she had. To scream as loud as she could and claw out his eyes. She settled for avoiding his question and slipping past him. But he grabbed an arm and her whole body tensed up.

"I want to know why it took you two fucking hours to call me," he said, tightening the grip on her arm.

"Because I didn't want to come home," she said. "You kicked me out of the car and called me a bitch. Or don't you remember?"

Aleksandr gave her a little shove as he released her. "Go get dressed for bed."

Clara walked out of the bathroom and froze when she saw the red lace slip laid out on the bed. She'd rather he just hit her again.

He walked out and placed his lips on her neck while holding her arms. "You said you were trying to be a better wife," he said into her ear. "I think it's time you kept your word." He ripped the towel from her and took it into the bathroom, leaving Clara standing naked in the middle of the room with tears trickling down her cheeks. Her hands trembled as she reached for the lingerie and slipped it on. It felt like poison on her skin.

She was still standing at the edge of the bed when Aleksandr came back into the room with his dress shirt unbuttoned. He grabbed a handful of her wet hair and pulled her head back to kiss her mouth. His tongue forced its way past her lips and she bit down on it, but the rebellious act had the opposite effect she'd been hoping. He pulled back with an evil grin on his face.

"Is this how we're going to play it?" he said.

And then like an angel sent down from the heavens, Aleksandr's phone started ringing and he frowned.

He pushed her down onto the bed as he moved to answer it, and she wiped her wet cheek with the back of her hand.

"*Shcho*," he answered.

She tuned him out as he continued the conversation in Ukrainian and prayed it was something that required his immediate attention.

Someone above was listening to her, because he ended the call in a huff and started buttoning up his shirt again.

"Nothing wrong, I hope," Clara said quietly.

Aleksandr just glared at her as he marched out of the room, slamming the door behind him. She continued to sit on the bed until she was sure he had left the house. When he was gone, she ran to the bathroom and vomited.

***

The phone rang and Aaron answered it in the first

[78]

ring.

"Clara," he said. "Are you all right?"

"I'm fine," she said. But her voice sounded shaky, weak.

"Are you sure?" Aaron asked. "Did he hurt you again?"

He heard her swallow hard before answering. "No. Really, I'm fine. I just wanted to call and check in. I know it's probably not smart right now."

"No, it's okay," he said. He had been imagining the worst since the moment she'd walked out of his sight and now it was a relief to hear her voice.

"Is Aleksandr there?" he asked.

"He's gone," she said. "He got a call a few minutes ago and had to rush out. I thought you were monitoring his phone."

"I am. But it hasn't had any activity all day."

"That's impossible. He was on it all morning and like I said, he just got a call this evening."

Dammit. Morozov must have gotten a new phone without Clara knowing. The question was, did he suspect something, or was he just being cautious?

"I probably just need to check things on my end," he told Clara. No point in scaring her any more than she already was.

"Oh." She went quiet and Aaron knew they should probably be getting off the line, but as long as she was on the phone with him, he knew she was safe.

"I should probably let you go," she said.

"You're probably right."

A few more minutes of silence and then Clara said, "Good night, Aaron."

"Good night, Clara. Be careful."

"You, too."

The line went dead and he put his head in his hands trying to remember the last time he'd felt so helpless.

***

The other side of the bed was still empty when Clara awoke the next morning. As she headed downstairs, she couldn't help but hope that Aleksandr had been involved in an accident and the cops would be arriving any minute to give her the tragic news. She was instead greeted by Ryan in the living room looking as cheerful as ever.

"Morning, Mrs. Morozov," he said. "Mr. Morozov asked me to let you know that he had to fly down to Las Vegas and should be back tonight or tomorrow."

"I see. And as usual he sent you over to babysit me in his absence."

"He just wants to make sure you're safe, ma'am."

"We both know that's bullshit," she said.

Ryan didn't respond and just looked down at his hands uncomfortably.

Clara sighed and felt sorry for the poor kid. "I have to run to the library, and then what do you say I treat you to lunch?" She was also hoping to see Aaron again.

He looked up at her with big round eyes. "Oh, Mr. Morozov asked that you don't leave the house today."

"He what? That's ridiculous! Why shouldn't I be able to leave my own house?"

"I don't know exactly, but it sounds like he's worried about something. Like there might be trouble brewing."

Clara wrinkled her brow, wondering what trouble that might be. The only trouble brewing was what she and Aaron were up to, and she didn't think she needed to be protected from herself.

"Well, I have some books that are due back," she lied. "You can either take me to the library or run them back yourself, leaving me here all by myself."

She could see the dilemma playing out on his face.

"I'm sure a quick trip to the library won't hurt anyone. But I'm afraid I'll have to say no to that lunch."

"Completely understandable," she said. "Let me go grab the books and I'll meet you in the car."

She ran into her room, picked a couple books she had no intention of reading anyway, and sent a message to Aaron letting her know she had limited time to meet him.

**

Aaron had rushed to the library as soon as he got Clara's message and was only there a couple minutes before she came bounding up the steps, looking as pleased to see him as he felt.

She joined him at the end of a stack and he pulled her into a corner where they were less visible so he could kiss her. Her body pressed against him, and he had to remember that they were in a public place.

"I only have two minutes," she said breathlessly when he finally let her go.

He pushed her hair back and gently touched the skin around the day old bruise. "Does it hurt?" he asked and she shook her head. "And you swear he didn't hurt you again last night?" She shook her head again, but there was something in her eyes. Something she didn't want to tell him. "Did he force you?" he whispered.

"No, He—No."

Aaron wrapped his arms around her and felt her whole body just melt into his. "Just say the word and you and I disappear."

She nodded into his chest. "I know," she said. He released her and she continued. "Listen, something is going on. Aleksandr rarely goes into Vegas, and suddenly he's flown down twice in a couple weeks. Both last minute trips."

"We're pretty sure he has some dealings down there, so it's not that unusual," said Aaron. "And if he's getting into human trafficking, that would be a good place to off-load a bunch of girls."

"And this morning, I practically had to beg Ryan to bring me here. My husband told him I wasn't to leave the house, and Ryan says he thinks there's trouble brewing. Do you think he's on to us?"

This was disturbing news. First Morozov switches out his phone and now he doesn't want Clara to leave the house. He looked down at her and saw the worry on her face.

"I don't know," he said and kissed her forehead. "But you should probably do as he says. Go home and sit tight."

She nodded.

"Call me, but only if you know it's absolutely safe."

"Of course," she said.

He gave her one last kiss, and with reluctance, watched her leave.

***

Clara woke in the middle of the night to loud voices. The clock read half-past two and she was worried. It was Aleksandr, but why was he yelling?

She grabbed a robe and descended the stairs to where he was going off on Ryan, who was on his knees and already had a black eye.

"Aleksandr!" she yelled. "What is going on?"

He spun around, and the anger in his eyes made her stop short halfway down the stairs. She then noticed two of his thugs also in the room and tightened the robe around her.

"You go back up to the room," he said. "I will deal with you next."

Clara's eyes moved from Aleksandr to Ryan and back to her husband. She was worried that if she didn't intervene, he was going to kill Ryan, but for what she had no idea. And what did he mean by deal with her? What did Aleksandr know?

"No," she said, moving to the bottom of the steps. The best defense was a good offense. "I won't have you beating up the poor kid in my living room. He needs ice."

Clara was scared shitless walking across the room to the kitchen, where she grabbed an ice pack from the freezer, but no one said anything when she came back out and kneeled in front of Ryan to press it to his eye. He winced, and although he didn't dare say it in front of Aleksandr, Clara saw the gratitude in his face.

"Now will you explain to me what he has done to deserve this?" she asked, hoping Aleksandr didn't decide to give her a black eye as well right then and there.

"You went to the library today," he said.

She swallowed hard. "So?"

"I told him you were not to leave the house."

"I still don't see what the big deal is," she said.

"I TOLD HIM YOU WERE NOT TO LEAVE THE HOUSE!" Aleksandr shouted, and both Clara and Ryan flinched.

She pulled the ice off to look at his eye that was starting to swell.

"Get your fucking hands off him, Clara," he said in an even, calm voice. Aleksandr's quiet scared her more than the shouting, and she handed Ryan the ice pack. Aleksandr grabbed her arm, yanking her off the floor.

"Take him away," he said, and the other two started dragging Ryan towards the door.

"Don't kill him," Clara begged as Aleksandr pulled her up the stairs. "Please don't kill him! This is my fault, I made him take me!" They turned a corner and she wondered if she would ever see Ryan again.

Aleksandr continued to say nothing until they were in the bedroom, where he slammed her against a wall.

"Why the hell do you care what happens to him?" Aleksandr spat at her. "Are you sleeping with him?"

"What?" she stuttered. "No, that's ridiculous!"

"Then why do you care?"

"Because I'm not like you," she said. "I don't like to see innocent people get hurt!"

"Ryan had one order," he said, pounding a finger into her chest, "and that was to keep you safe."

"Let's not pretend that you give a shit about my

[85]

safety," she screamed at him.

Aleksandr slapped her. "I have loved you and done nothing but take care of you. How dare you question my motives!"

Clara touched her cheek and spoke softly. "Well you have a funny way of showing it."

He growled and shook her briefly before letting her go. "Get dressed and start packing. We leave in an hour."

"Leaving?" she asked. "Where are we going?" She did not like this at all.

"Somewhere safe," he said, pulling a suitcase out of the closet.

"Safe from what?"

"Just shut up and do as I say!"

This was bad. Clara knew this was really bad. She needed to get a message to Aaron, but it was going to be impossible if Aleksandr didn't leave her side.

CHAPTER SIX

It had been more than twenty-four hours since Aaron had left Clara at the library and he was worried. He was sure that she would have called by now. It was risky, but he decided to try her cell.

It rang several times, and just when he thought it would go to voicemail, someone picked up. But it wasn't who he was hoping for.

"Who is this?" growled Morozov.

"Hey," said Aaron, thinking quickly. "I was looking for my buddy, John. Is he around?"

"There's no John here. Don't ever call this number again." The line went dead.

"God damn it!" Aaron swore as he threw the phone onto the bed.

***

"Who's John?" Aleksandr asked Clara, who was

staring out the window down onto the streets of Vegas. "Who's calling your phone?"

"I don't know," she said, turning to him. "I don't know any John."

He smacked her across the face, causing her to fall against a chair where her hip made contact with the solid arm.

"Don't lie to me," he shouted.

Her tongue ran across her lip, tasting blood where it had split.

"I swear to you I don't know any John!" she said, not looking him in the eye. She may not know any John, but she knew exactly who had called her phone.

Aleksandr grabbed a fistful of hair and pulled her head back.

"Why don't I believe you?" he asked. But there was a knock at the door and Aleksandr pushed her onto the floor.

"What?" he asked, opening the door.

"It's time."

Aleksandr pocketed her phone and walked into the living area of their two bedroom penthouse suite at the Aria. Clara picked herself up off the floor and moved to the doorway, clutching her bruised hip to watch him gather all his men except Sergei.

"You make sure she stays in here, and no one is to enter," he told Sergei. "Understood?"

"Sure, Boss," said Sergei.

"Where are you going?" she asked him. "When can I go home?"

"Where I'm going is none of your business," he said. "And this is our home now."

Clara's jaw dropped.

"Let's go," he said to the three men awaiting his orders.

"What is he talking about?" she asked Sergei. "What does he mean this is our home now?"

But he just shrugged, which was as much as she expected. She turned around and slammed the bedroom door behind her only to have Sergei open it.

"I'd prefer that you keep this open, ma'am," he said.

"Why? Are you afraid I might try to break the window and jump thirty stories?"

"Let's just keep it open, please."

Clara sighed and plopped on the bed. She again felt the bruise on her hip and went into the bathroom to take a better look at it. As she was looking at it in the mirror, she noticed the telephone by the toilet. What if she tried to call Aaron from the room phone? She stepped out and could hear that Sergei had turned on the television.

"I'm taking a shower," she called out. "Can I at least close my bathroom door?"

"Fine," he shouted back.

She closed the door, turned on the water, and

dialed Aaron's number.

It went to voicemail and she realized he probably wasn't going to answer a number he didn't recognize, especially after having just reached Aleksandr.

"Aaron, it's me," she said. "Obviously you can't call my cell anymore, but we're at the Aria in Vegas. I don't know what's going on, but he says this is our home now. Aaron, I'm scared." Clara found herself on the verge of tears as the words tumbled out of her. "I want out, I don't know what's going to happen, please come get me." She hung up the phone and prayed it wasn't too late.

***

Aaron's leg bounced nervously under the table as he waited for Gavin to arrive. A glance at his watch showed it had only been twenty minutes since he had sent the message, but it felt much longer. And every minute that passed had him imagining worse and worse things happening to Clara.

When Gavin finally sauntered in fifteen minutes later, Aaron strained to keep his voice even.

"Took you long enough," he said.

"Do you think I sit around all day waiting for you to send a message?"

"We need to get Clara Morozov out," said Aaron. He didn't have time to waste arguing.

"And why is that?"

"I got a message from her less than an hour ago.

She's in Vegas and is scared. She's asked to be extracted."

"We still don't have what we need," said Gavin.

"Screw that," said Aaron, pounding a fist into the table. Several diners looked in their direction and he lowered his voice before continuing. "She is an innocent civilian requesting our protection."

"Then tell her to call the cops, but we can't intervene until we're ready to take Morozov down or he'll get spooked."

"The cops aren't going to fucking help," said Aaron. "Even if she did manage to call them, they won't get within twenty feet of her. Morozov will kill her before they do."

"My hands are tied, Wells. We have our own problems to deal with."

"What are you talking about?"

"Well, for one, the container is due to arrive tomorrow," said Gavin, "and it sounds like you're telling me Morozov isn't even in the state. How are we supposed to bust him in a sting if he's not even around?"

"Shit," Aaron muttered.

"And we've managed to figure out where all the containers are headed after they come in. Most are staying in the area, a few are headed to Montana and beyond, but not a single container on the ship is destined for Las Vegas."

Aaron's brow creased. "That can't be right. Maybe it's taking a roundabout course. Trying to throw us off guard."

"We've exhausted a lot of manpower, but every container on that ship has been accounted for."

Aaron put his head in his hands, trying to sort out what this could mean.

"Are you sure you can trust her?" Gavin asked, and Aaron's head snapped back up.

"Yes. Without a doubt. This is a woman living in fear. I have seen the bruises her husband has inflicted."

Gavin sighed. "Then I don't know what to tell you."

"She saw the packing slip, she saw the date and country of origin."

"Did she see for sure that its destination was Seattle?" Gavin asked.

"I'm not sure," Aaron said slowly. "I suppose it's possible she missed that part and we both just assumed it was coming into Seattle."

"So we have a ship coming in from Hong Kong tomorrow that could be sailing into any one of the twenty plus west coast ports."

"If it's headed to Las Vegas we can probably assume it's going into California."

"Great, that narrows the list down to ten," said Gavin. "At this point, it doesn't matter. There's no way for us to weed through all the potential containers by tomorrow."

"What am I supposed to tell Clara then? That because she missed the part about what city the ship was going into, she's screwed?"

Gavin shrugged. "If you can get a message to her, tell her to walk away as soon as she can, whether she has to call the cops or not."

Aaron's nostrils flared as he stared Gavin right in the eye. "The last time she tried to walk away, Morozov put her in the ER and cost her her unborn child."

"I get what you're saying, but the agency can't get involved."

"Fuck you, Maxwell. And the agency," Aaron said, getting up and heading for the door.

"Don't do anything stupid, Wells," Gavin called after him.

***

Aaron killed the engine of his bike and yanked off his helmet. It was career suicide, but Aaron knew he couldn't leave Clara to fend for herself. He couldn't abandon her. It was time to call the one person that could help him pull off a job like this.

"Hello?" said a female voice on the other end.

"Jillian? It's Aaron. How are you?"

"Aaron? Wow, haven't heard from you in a while."

"Yeah, I've been busy. Listen, is Reid around?"

"Yeah, he's here. Hold on."

"Wells," said Reid. "How are you, man?"

"I've been better. Listen Jackson, I hate to do this, but I need to call in a favor."

***

Aaron sat on the edge of an empty baggage carousel at McCarran Airport. When Reid finally came down the escalator, Aaron picked up the bag sitting at his feet and greeted his old partner with a big hug and slap on the back.

"Thanks for coming out, Jackson," said Aaron.

"Happy to return the favor," said Reid. "Though I have to admit, I never thought I'd see the day Aaron Wells went soft for a girl."

"It's not like that. She needs our help."

"Of course," said Reid, giving him a wink.

"How's Jillian?" Aaron asked as they made their way out of the airport.

"She's good. But not too happy about me being here. Said to tell you if you don't send me back in one piece she'll have to hunt you down."

Aaron laughed. "I'll keep that in mind."

"She also said to tell you to come by sometime."

Aaron raised an eyebrow. He doubted Jillian cared one way or the other. Not that he blamed her.

"I've been busy," he said.

"I know. And I'm sorry."

Aaron knew he was apologizing for leaving, and

for the first time he was ready to forgive Reid. He finally understood.

"I know," he said.

"So where're we headed?" Reid asked once they had secured a rental car.

"She's at the Aria."

***

It had been two hours since Clara had left the message for Aaron, and she had spent most of the time curled up on her bed wondering if there was really anything he could do for her now. She wished she had taken him up on his offer back at the apartment.

The front door opened and she sat up as Aleksandr came into the room, carrying her handbag.

"Come with me," he said, holding out his hand.

Clara took it and climbed off the bed. "Where are we going?" she asked, trembling. Was this it? Were they going somewhere where no one would ever find her body?

"It's a surprise," he said, smiling. "Something I've been working on for a while now."

She followed him down to the lobby and out to valet where a black Land Rover was waiting for them. Her fears worsened as they drove out of the city, but then they pulled up to a large house and Aleksandr helped her out of the vehicle.

"Welcome to your new home," he said.

"I don't understand," she said.

"I'm moving my business down here. We're done with Seattle. It's getting, well, let's just say I'm not comfortable up there anymore. And I've found better opportunities down here."

Clara stood there, just staring at the front door, wondering what to make of it all.

"Do you want to look around?" he asked.

"Why have you not talked to me about this? Why all the secrecy?"

Aleksandr unlocked the door and pulled her into the massive foyer with a rounded staircase on her left. This house was huge, probably twice the size of their Bellevue home.

"I wanted to surprise you," he said. "It's not safe for us in Seattle anymore. The death of my brothers showed that, so I've spent the past two years building my empire elsewhere."

Clara thought it odd he only mentioned his brothers, but then Aleksandr had never really been close to his father. "But what about the rest of your family in Seattle? Will they all move down here as well?" She followed him as he wandered the still-empty house with a look of pride on his face.

"I'm not cutting ties with Seattle entirely. Yurik and Stephan will run things there. With my guidance, of course. Think of this as more of an expansion of my empire."

He led her up the stairs, but Clara wasn't really seeing the house.

"And does this expansion include human trafficking?" she asked.

Aleksandr narrowed his eyes at her, but it was a much milder reaction than she had been expecting. "Who told you that?"

She shrugged. "I hear things."

He cupped her chin tightly and lifted it so that her eyes met his. "I don't think I need to remind you that it would be best to keep your nose out of my affairs."

"So it's true then."

The house must have put him in a good mood, because he simply ignored her comment and motioned her into one of the oversized bedrooms.

"I thought this one would make a good nursery," he said. "It's the closest one to the master."

She looked around it and could indeed imagine a crib against the wall, a rocking chair over by the window. But even if she could have children, she would never let Aleksandr anywhere near them.

"Don't you agree?" he asked when she didn't say anything.

She nodded at him and walked out of the room.

"We should go," he said, looking at his watch. "We are expected for lunch."

***

The Range Rover pulled up to a brand new

restaurant that didn't even look open for business yet.

"Welcome to Kattrina's," said Aleksandr. "After my mother, of course. The grand opening is this weekend."

It was true that Clara had tried to keep out of her husband's way, but she was still shocked by how much he had accomplished without her knowledge. A new house and new restaurant? What else did he have in store for her?

They walked in and she followed Aleksandr to the back room, where she looked right into the eyes of a ghost.

"Dimitre," she whispered.

Aleksandr's father lifted a small glass of vodka to her. "Hello, Clara. It's so good to see you again."

CHAPTER SEVEN

"But you're dead," she said. "I was at your funeral."

Both men laughed in a way that made Clara feel stupid.

"Well I'm glad you believed it," said Dimitre, sipping his vodka. "It was a good plan, no?"

"I don't understand," she said.

"Please, sit." Dimitre sat at a round table identical to the one in the Seattle restaurant, and Aleksandr held out a chair for Clara, but she didn't want to sit. She wanted to run away. Dimitre being alive could not be a good thing. She started to take a step back, but Aleksandr grabbed her shoulder and forced her into the chair before seating himself between her and his father.

"It is true that I almost died," said Dimitre. "I still

have the shrapnel in my chest." He prodded to the left of his heart. "It was Aleksandr here who decided to let everyone believe that I didn't make it." He slapped Aleksandr on the back, and she could see the pride on both their faces. "He paid the right people and a body was buried, but it was not mine."

The two men raised their glasses in a toast.

"To second chances," said Dimitre.

"*Da*," Aleksandr agreed.

"And you've been down here all this time," said Clara, "helping him to relocate."

"Police have been getting too close in Seattle. Even now, they watch you up there."

Dimitre's words rattled Clara. "But that's nothing new," she said, hoping her pitch wasn't too high. "The family has always been watched."

He waved a hand. "No matter. It was time to move on."

"Why are you telling me all this?" she asked, unable to keep the shakiness out of her voice this time.

Dimitre lit a cigar and took a couple deep puffs before answering. She noticed even Aleksandr was looking uncomfortable.

"Grab her wrists," Dimitre said.

She looked at Aleksandr as he stood and grabbed her hands from behind, pinning them palms up on the table.

"What are you doing?" she asked in fear.

"Who have you been talking to, Clara?" Dimitre asked.

"I don't understand."

He tapped his cigar over her left wrist, causing the hot ashes to settle on her skin, and she blew at them.

"Someone hacked Aleksandr's phone. I'm guessing an inside job. And who is closer to my son than you?"

"It wasn't me," she said with tears welling in her eyes. "I would never do something like that! I wouldn't even know how."

The cigar was pushed into her wrist and Clara screamed as the flesh melted beneath it. Aleksandr's grip only tightened as she tried to pull her hands away.

"Who have you been talking to?" Dimitre shouted when he pulled the cigar away.

"No one," Clara sobbed. They would kill her if they knew she was lying, so she figured she might as well die protecting Aaron. "I would never betray Aleksandr."

Dimitre took the cigar to her again and she screamed louder, fought Aleksandr even harder, almost breaking free, but he would always be stronger than her.

"Isn't it true that you tried to leave my son when you were pregnant with his child?" Dimitre asked.

Tears were streaming down Clara's cheeks as she

smelled her own burning flesh, but she looked in Dimitre's eyes and this time told him the truth.

"Of course I did," she cried. "Because your son beats me and I was scared not only for my life, but the life of my unborn child! I was scared, but I was never going to betray him. I just wanted to get away from him."

Dimitre sneered and started to press the cigar again, but Aleksandr let Clara's hands go.

"Enough," he said. "She's clearly telling the truth." If she hadn't been in so much pain, Clara would have laughed at the irony. It was okay for Aleksandr to hurt her whenever he saw fit, but to see someone else do the job was a different matter.

Dimitre looked at them both with skepticism but said nothing.

"I told you it was Ryan, her driver," Aleksandr said.

Dimitre flicked his cigar into an ashtray this time. "And you have dealt with this traitor?"

Aleksandr did not answer his father, but the tense glance in Clara's direction was the only answer she needed.

"Oh, God," she said, feeling even more sick. "Not Ryan!" she shouted at him. Working for her had not been as risk-free as he had hoped. And it was all her fault.

"Get her out of here," he said as Clara sat across

from him clutching her wrist and crying. Aleksandr pulled her out of the chair and grabbed the gauze from the counter that she realized must have been sitting there the whole time.

In the car, she let Aleksandr wrap her wrist.

"I'm sorry, Clara," he said. "But we had to be sure."

He tried to put an arm around her, but she pushed it off.

"One day you'll understand," he told her.

The fuck I will, she thought. *If Aaron can't help me, I may just kill the bastard myself. Both of them.*

***

The driver dropped them off at the front entrance, and as they were entering the lobby, Clara noticed a man on the phone across the floor looking right at her. Even when she caught his eye, he didn't stop staring at her. She looked at Aleksandr, but he was too absorbed in the conversation on his own phone to notice anything. The stranger was tall with sandy-colored hair and striking blue eyes and was heading right in her direction. Suddenly he flashed her a quick smile and winked just before knocking right into her, causing her bag to fall and spill across the floor.

"I am so sorry, miss," he said, helping her gather her items.

"Um, thanks," she said.

"I believe this is yours as well," he said, handing her a copy of *Anna Karenina*. It even had the King County library barcode on it.

Aaron.

"Yes. Yes it is," she said, feeling hopeful for the first time all day.

"What's going on here?" Aleksandr asked, finally noticing his wife was no longer in step with him.

The tall stranger apologized again and took off out the front doors.

Clara tucked the thick book into her now cramped purse and followed Aleksandr the rest of the way to the room.

***

"Package has been delivered," said Reid's voice over the phone.

"How did she look?" Aaron asked.

"I could see her husband's handiwork," Reid answered.

"When I saw her yesterday all she had was a bruise."

"Well, now she has a cut lip and her left wrist was bandaged."

"Dammit," Aaron muttered. "Head back up and we'll figure out the next step. But every minute she stays with him she's in danger."

"Got it," said Reid and he hung up.

***

As soon as they walked into the room, Aleksandr went to the bar to pour himself a drink, and Clara bee-lined it for the bedroom. She took her bag into the bathroom, locked the door behind her, and pulled the book out. She held it spine up and tried to shake out any message that might be in it, but nothing fell out. There was nothing obviously written on it, yet Clara was sure it had a message for her. She started fanning the pages looking for anything out of the ordinary. Nothing stood out, but a couple of pages had stuck together. She tried again and swore that the same two pages were sticking together. It took a little effort to get them pulled apart, and she saw why. Tucked between these two pages was the note she had been looking for, and it was no accident that they were sticking together. The corners of the page were tacky, with what she didn't know, but it was obviously done intentionally in case Aleksandr had done what she had first done, looking for a note to fall out.

I'm in room 14008, the note said, *I will find you.*

Clara held the note to her chest and closed her eyes. Aaron was here, he was close.

A knock at the door made her jump.

"Clara, you in there?" said Aleksandr.

She stood up and started tearing the note up, throwing it into the toilet.

"I'm going to the bathroom. Just give me a

minute." She flushed the toilet and watched to make sure every last piece went down the drain before washing her hands in the sink. She started to unlock the door, then decided to shove the book back in her bag still sitting on the counter.

Aleksandr pounded on the door. "What's taking you so long?"

She opened the door and proceeded to pull a lipstick out of her bag to reapply. "I told you, I was going to the bathroom."

"I have medicine for you," he said.

She was confused until she saw the ointment and fresh gauze in his hand. "Oh," she said. "You mean for the burns your father inflicted on me."

He took her wrist and unwrapped the bandage, revealing the ugly burn that needed more than just some ointment.

"I can do it myself," she told him and tried to pull her hand out of his grasp.

"Let me," he said. "Please."

A million thoughts went through Clara's head. Things she wanted to say to Aleksandr. But Aaron was close, and she wouldn't have to deal with her husband much longer.

***

The phone rang in room 14008, and Aaron held his breath as Reid answered it.

"I think it's Clara," Reid whispered as he handed it

[106]

to Aaron.

"Clara," he said into the mouthpiece.

"Oh, Aaron," she said, "it's so good to hear your voice."

"Where are you?" he asked.

"I'm in my room. Locked in the bathroom. As usual." She chuckled, but it sounded forced.

"You're not alone then?"

"No," she said. "Aleksandr keeps a man on me at all times, and I only get to leave the room with him apparently."

"What happened to your wrist?" he asked.

"My wrist? How do you know about that?"

"Reid, my partner…he said he saw your wrist was bandaged. What did the asshole do to you?"

"That wasn't Aleksandr," she said. "Although he did help."

"Help who? Clara what happened?"

"Dimitre Morozov used my wrist as an ashtray."

Aaron must have misheard her. "Did you say *Dimitre* Morozov? As in Aleksandr's father?"

"The one and only."

"But he's dead. He was killed two years ago."

"I assure you he is alive and well. I have the burns to prove it."

"What the hell is going on?"

"It turns out—" But she was cut off. "Shit. I have to go." There was a click and the line went dead.

[107]

***

Clara hung up the phone and opened the bathroom door. She was starting to think of this room as a second home to her.

"What?" she asked Sergio, who had been pounding on the door.

"Were you on the phone?"

She screwed up her face. "What? No, I was going to the bathroom."

"I thought I saw a light on the phone in the living room," he said. "Are you sure you weren't using it?"

"Of course I'm sure," she said, pushing past him. "Why would I make a phone call while sitting on the toilet?" She sat down on the bed and picked up the phone next to it. "But I was planning on ordering room service. Did you want anything?"

At the mention of food, Sergio's face lit up and she had to refrain from rolling her eyes at how predictable he was. The man was without a doubt hired for his muscles.

***

Aaron hung up the phone, still trying to process what Clara had just told him.

"Dimitre Morozov is alive," he said to Reid.

"A relation to Aleksandr Morozov, I'm assuming."

"It's his father," said Aaron. "He died from the blast of a car bomb that killed his two older sons. Or so we thought. But according to Clara, she was with him. Tortured by him even."

"What does this mean?" Reid asked.

Aaron ran a thumb along his lower jaw. "I'm not really sure. Can't be good though."

"What about Clara?"

"She's under constant guard in her room," said Aaron.

"Well that complicates things," said Reid. "Not impossible, just more complicated."

"It never is easy."

"Just like old times."

Aaron grinned. "Just like old times."

***

The front door opened just as Clara got off the phone with room service. Aleksandr walked into the room holding a garment bag and a shoe box.

"Get dressed," he said, dropping the items on the bed.

She unzipped the bag to reveal a signature bandage dress by Herve Leger.

"Where exactly are we going that I need to wear this?" she asked.

"To a club," he said.

"And since when do we go clubbing?"

"Since I bought one."

"Jesus, Aleksandr," she said with wide eyes. "Did you buy up all of Las Vegas while I wasn't looking?"

A small smile appeared on his face. "Not yet. Now

hurry up and get dressed."

"But I just ordered room service," she said. "I'm starving."

"Hopefully it arrives before we leave."

Clara sighed and took the bag and shoes into the bathroom. As she squeezed into the one-shoulder dress, she wondered why he always did this to her. It was sure to garner the attention of other men, and once again, he would accuse her of being a whore. She closed her eyes, took a deep breath, and exhaled slowly. She just needed to be patient.

She was in the middle of applying makeup, trying to cover up the fading bruise, when he walked in. His reflection in the mirror stared back at her progress.

"The club is dark enough," he said. "I'm sure no one will notice."

Her eyes shot daggers at him, but he ignored it as he pulled a blue box from behind his back.

"One more thing," he said.

She turned to face him, and he opened the box to reveal a Tiffany's four-row pearl bracelet. Clara imagined so many women would be thrilled to be accepting such a gift from their husbands, but she only saw it as obscene. And she knew exactly why he had bought it.

Aleksandr pulled the bracelet from the box and clasped it around her left wrist, all but covering up the gauze wrapped around it. As with every other wound inflicted on her, Aleksandr always bought something beautiful to cover it up. Designer sunglasses, silk scarves, whatever was needed. His hand brushed her cheek and he kissed her.

"You look beautiful," he said.

She reached back and gripped the counter behind her, resisting the urge to hit him. "Thanks," she whispered.

Someone rapped on the bedroom door. "Food's here," they said.

"You're in luck," said Aleksandr.

But Clara had lost her appetite.

***

Inspiration struck when Clara spotted the hotel note pad and pen on the desk as Aleksandr gave directions to his men.

"Sergio, you will ride with us in the Rover," he said. "The rest of you go now and make sure it's clear. We'll be right behind you."

Clara set her purse on the table, pretending to make sure she had everything she needed, and tucked the pen and paper into it while everyone was bustling about.

"Clara, are you ready?" Aleksandr asked.

"All set," she said, snapping her purse closed.

"So what's the name of this club that you now own?" she asked as they stepped into the elevator.

"Club Noir," he said.

"Club Noir. I like it," she said, trying to keep the mood pleasant.

Aleksandr put his arm around her and gave a squeeze. "Las Vegas will be a new start for us. You'll see."

She forced a smile.

***

They stepped off the elevator and cut across the casino floor towards the front entrance.

"I meant to use the restroom before I left," said Clara. "Do you mind if I duck in before we get in the car?"

Aleksandr rolled his eyes but waved his hand. "Go, but hurry."

"I will."

She swooped into the women's bathroom and pulled out the pen and paper to write Aaron a quick note saying where she would be. She folded it in half and wrote the room number on it. A woman was drying her hands, and Clara approached her.

"Hi, I have a huge favor to ask," she said. "Could you run this over to the concierge? It's just across the floor. Have them deliver it to this room?" She pointed to the number on it.

"Sure." The woman looked pleased to be helping out.

"Thanks. And make sure they deliver it right away. I can't tell you how much I appreciate it."

"Not a problem," the woman said.

"I have to run. Again, thank you!"

Clara quickly exited the bathroom and followed her husband out to where the Rover was waiting for them.

***

"So what's our best way of getting to the room?" Reid asked Aaron as they looked over schematics of the hotel.

"Well, the Sky Suites have their own elevator, so we either need to steal a key card, or we could use service outlets."

"It might be easier to get into the room pretending to be hotel employees," said Reid.

"I was just thinking that."

A knock at the door put both men on alert, grabbing their guns. Aaron looked into the peephole to see a male hotel employee standing on the other side. He held up a finger and Reid pocketed his gun, but Aaron kept his cocked and hid behind the door as Reid cracked it open.

"Yes," he said.

"I was asked to deliver this message to you right away," said the man, handing Reid a note.

"Thanks." Reid took it and closed the door. "It's from Clara," he said, handing it to Aaron.

Aaron read it and looked up at Reid. "Looks like opportunity may have knocked on our door."

CHAPTER EIGHT

The Rover dropped them off at the back entrance to Club Noir, and they were let in by a sharply-dressed man wearing too much hair gel for Clara's liking.

"Good evening, Mr. Morozov," he said. "A pleasure to see you again."

Aleksandr nodded. "Oscar Santiago, this is my wife, Clara."

Oscar took her hand with both hands, and she knew he was already undressing her with his eyes. "It is a pleasure to meet you, *Señorita.*"

"I believe *señora* is the word you're looking for," she said, glancing at her husband.

Oscar laughed, revealing unnaturally white teeth. "Ah, you got me," he said and released her hand. "Mr. Morozov is a very lucky man indeed."

"Oscar is the general manager here," said

Aleksandr. "Tonight he's going to demonstrate why I should keep him on under the new ownership."

Clara had a feeling he wasn't going to last long.

"*Sí.* Now, if you will follow me."

Oscar led the group up a flight of stairs to an office that had a glass wall overlooking the club floor, presumably mirrored on the club side. Clara moved to it as Oscar flipped on a computer screen. The club was open, but mostly empty due to the early hour.

"Sergio," Aleksandr called from the desk. "Why don't you take my wife downstairs? No need to bore her with business."

Clara sighed as she followed Sergio back downstairs. An elevated VIP section was roped off, and the men who had come before them were already seated here with a bottle of vodka.

She and Sergio sat down among them, and a server came over to take ask if they needed anything else.

"Just cranberry juice for me, please. In a high ball glass, if you don't mind."

The server nodded and walked away.

Clara wanted to keep a clear head in case Aaron got her note in time.

***

An hour later, the club was starting to fill up and Clara was bored as hell when Aleksandr finally came down the stairs with Oscar, who split off to make the rounds. Everyone made room for Aleksandr to sit next to Clara, and he poured himself a drink from the bottle service.

"This is nice, isn't it?" he said to Clara, and she nodded. "What are you drinking?"

"Vodka and cranberry," she lied.

Aleksandr frowned. "It looks too weak." He added vodka to her cranberry juice. "You should be enjoying yourself!" he said.

"I wouldn't want to overdo it and make a fool of myself," she said.

He turned his attention to one of the men, and Clara set her untouched drink on the table. She scanned the crowd dancing to the heavy bass blaring from the speakers. And then she saw him at the bar. The tall guy with the striking blue eyes. He raised his glass slightly in her direction and gave a nod towards the restrooms.

She looked at the men surrounding her, none of whom were paying any attention to her, and stood up. Aleksandr grabbed her arm.

"Where are you going?" he asked.

"I have to pee."

"Sergio," he barked.

"Seriously?"

"Go with her, Sergio."

Sergio nodded and stood to follow her.

She rolled her eyes and stepped down to the dance floor, pushing past people to get to the bathroom. At the edge of the floor, Blue Eyes slipped by and whispered in her ear.

"Go out the back, black Charger waiting. I'll run interference."

She nodded once and kept moving. As she neared the restrooms, she turned back to see him and Sergio in conversation. It was hard to imagine what they were talking about, but Sergio wasn't watching her anymore, so she ducked towards the back door, almost breaking into a run.

A blast of cool night air hit her as the door swung out. The Charger was waiting, just as Blue Eyes had said it would be, with the passenger door open. And there was Aaron in the front seat.

**

"Get in!" Aaron shouted the second he saw Clara come bursting through the back door.

She jumped in and slammed the door.

"We have to get Reid," he said, driving around to the front.

"Who?" she asked.

"Reid, my partner."

"Oh, Blue Eyes."

Aaron risked a glance at her and smiled. "Yeah, Blue Eyes."

They pulled up to the front door where Reid was waiting, and he slid into the back seat the second Aaron slowed down enough.

"That was a lot easier than I thought it would be," said Reid as they peeled off.

"What were you talking to him about?" Clara asked.

"I asked him how he got his arms so big, and he started blabbing about his workout and protein shakes."

"Of course he did," she said.

"I'm pretty sure he thinks you're still in the bathroom," said Reid.

Clara turned to Aaron and grinned. "Aleksandr is going to be pissed at him when he realizes I'm gone."

Aaron reached over and took her hand. "I told you all you had to do was say the word."

"Yes, you did," she said softly, and it was all Aaron could do not to stop the car right then and there and take her into his arms.

"I'm Reid, by the way," came his partner's voice from the back seat.

Clara released Aaron's hand and twisted in her seat. "I'm Clara. Thank you so much for all your help today."

"No problem," said Reid. "I owed Aaron."

"I see," she said. "So where to now?"

"There's a safehouse about an hour out," said Aaron. "We'll spend the night there and figure out what's next. Is that okay?"

"Anywhere away from my husband is just fine

with me," she said.

Aaron set the cruise control to eighty and drove away from the bright lights, out into the night.

***

Clara's eyes flew open as the car hit a bump. She must have fallen asleep. The last thing she remembered was slouching down into the passenger seat as Aaron took her hand again. A glance showed that he was still holding it, and Clara gave a squeeze.

"Hey," he said quietly. "We're getting close."

She sat up and saw that they were traveling along a gravel road in what appeared to be the middle of nowhere. She turned around and saw Reid texting on his phone in the darkness.

"Who you talking to?" she asked, hearing the grogginess in her voice.

"Jillian," he said. "My girlfriend. Well, technically my fiancée."

"Wait, your fiancée?" said Aaron. "Since when?"

"Since last week," said Reid.

"That's sweet," Clara said, smiling. "Congratulations."

"Thanks."

"Were you ever going to tell me?" asked Aaron.

"I was hoping you'd be my best man," said Reid.

Clara watched Aaron's expression go from annoyed to humbled.

"Really?" he asked.

"Of course," said Reid. "I didn't say anything sooner because it didn't feel appropriate until now."

"Wow, I'd be honored," said Aaron. "We're here," he said suddenly as they pulled up to a small cabin situated in a grove of pine trees.

***

Aaron killed the engine and popped the trunk. Everyone exited the vehicle, and Reid grabbed a bag from the back. Clara followed Aaron to the front porch, where he found a loose board and pulled out a small box containing the key.

He opened the front door but held Clara back, letting Reid in first to do a sweep of the one-bedroom structure. Once he nodded to them, Aaron walked in with Clara. He looked around at the sparse furnishings, then back to Clara who was standing near the couch, shivering in just her heels and tight black dress. He grabbed a quilt from the bedroom and wrapped it around her. The shimmer on her wrist caught his attention.

"Sit down and let me take a look," he said, pulling her onto the couch with him. She held her left arm out and he unclasped the bracelet before gingerly removing the bandaging.

"Jesus Christ," he muttered. It was worse than he had imagined. "Does it hurt?" She nodded. "And you're telling me Morozov held you down while his father did this to you?" She nodded again, and this time her eyes started to well up.

Aaron wrapped his arms around her, careful of the hand.

"He will never hurt you again," he said into her ear. "Do you understand? Never again."

She nodded into his chest and gave a sniff before pulling away, and Aaron looked at the wound again.

"This doesn't look good; we're going to need to clean it out."

"I know," she said.

"Reid, is there a medical kit somewhere with hydrogen peroxide or something?"

"Should be," said Reid. He rummaged through the kitchen cabinets until he found what he was looking for.

Aaron led Clara over to the kitchen and had her hold her hand over the sink as he opened the bottles of hydrogen peroxide and rubbing alcohol.

"We'll do the peroxide first to help clean out the wound," said Aaron, "and then we'll do the alcohol to make sure there's no infection. It's going to hurt though."

"I'm ready," she said. "Let's get this over with."

He poured the peroxide over it, causing her to inhale sharply as the wound bubbled and became frothy. A couple more times and then he poured the alcohol over it. Clara screwed up her face and bit her lip, but she made no sound. The woman was tough as nails. Once it was dry enough, he found some ointment and bandaged her up again.

"Better?" Aaron asked, kissing her palm.

"Much," she said. "Now I don't suppose you have something for me to wear other than this dress."

"Think I have a t-shirt you can borrow," he said.

"I'll take it."

***

Clara walked out of the bathroom feeling much more comfortable with a scrubbed face and wearing Aaron's shirt. She loved being wrapped up in his scent. She joined him and Reid huddled on the couch and pulled the quilt back around her shoulders.

"So what's the plan?" she asked. "Where do we go from here?"

"Well, the first stop will be to get Reid home," said Aaron. "And then we go into hiding."

Clara frowned. "What about Aleksandr? How long until they take him into custody?"

When Aaron didn't immediately answer, she knew something was wrong.

"What's changed?" she said. "I thought you had everything you needed."

"It turns out the container wasn't going into Seattle," said Aaron. "By the time we figured it out, there wasn't enough time to pinpoint it. It would have arrived today, and we have no way to link it to him."

Clara felt like the room was spinning. "So everything I did," she said, "was for nothing. All that and I still have to spend the rest of my life running from him."

Aaron reached for her hand. "I'm so sorry, Clara."

"And what do you mean by hiding? Won't your agency give me protection at least?"

"I'm afraid not," he said. "They were worried that any involvement on their part would jeopardize the whole operation."

"But they sent you guys here to get me."

Aaron said nothing

"Didn't they?" she asked.

"No. Reid isn't even with the agency anymore. When I told them you wanted out, they recommended you call the local authorities."

"What?" Clara couldn't believe what she was hearing. "Call the cops? Did they really think that was going to work in my favor? They do know who my husband is, right?"

"That's what I told my supervisor."

What Aaron was saying clicked in her mind. "But you came for me anyway," she said softly.

"Of course I did."

There was no doubt in Clara's mind that she loved this man sitting in front of her. After all the bullshit, pain, and hell she had been through, Aaron had been willing to move mountains to take her out of it.

"Thank you."

"Unfortunately," Reid chimed in, "that means Aaron broke a direct order. He probably just fucked up a whole operation by going in for you."

"I didn't fuck anything up," said Aaron. "The damn operation was going nowhere once the container lead went cold. But he's right. I did disobey an order, which means I can't go back either without risking jail time."

Guilt swept over Clara. "I never wanted that for you," she said.

"Hey," he said, taking her hand. "Don't worry about it. I wouldn't have done it if I didn't feel it was worth it. Every minute with him was a minute too long."

"So what do we do now?" Clara asked again.

"I've got a contact making up papers now; we just need to get some fresh passport photos before we meet up with him in New York. Then we can go wherever you want. I suggest somewhere out of the country though."

"And just like that, we'll disappear." Saying it out loud didn't make it feel any more real.

"Just like that," Aaron repeated. "I think we should color your hair and maybe get some color contacts."

"To make it harder to find me," she said.

The anxiety must have been showing on her face, because he took her face in both his hands and said,

"We don't have to do it right now. We can't fly right now, especially since you have no ID on you, but it wouldn't be safe anyway. So we've got two days, three at most for you to think about what you want to do."

She stared into his dark brown eyes without saying anything.

"Tell me what's going through your head right now," he asked.

What was going through her head at the moment was how this had been exactly what she didn't want. She didn't want to go into hiding. To have to always worry if Aleksandr was going to find her. But it had to be better than a life *with* Aleksandr.

"You'll be with me," she said out loud.

"Yes. You and me together."

"Then I'm fine."

Aaron smiled at her.

"I think I'm going to turn in now." She wasn't sure if she would be able to sleep, but Clara needed to lie down and process all of this.

"All right. Reid and I just have to discuss a few more details."

Clara walked into the bedroom and slid under the covers. They had never discussed sleeping arrangements, but she knew Aaron would be joining her soon.

*****

"She's freaking out," Reid said as Aaron watched Clara disappear into the bedroom.

"You think," said Aaron.

"Jillian did too when I told her she couldn't go home right away."

"I still maintain that men in our profession don't do relationships."

Reid shrugged. "I said the same thing. But it's too late now."

"Let's just finish up here," said Aaron.

They spent the next few minutes making a plan to leave before the sun came up, and what path they would take.

"We'll have you home in time for dinner," Aaron told Reid, "and then Clara and I should be in New York by evening next day, barring any obstacles."

"So what you're saying is we're going to have to have a destination wedding if you're going to attend," said Reid.

"I'm sure I could find a way to sneak back in the country for a weekend."

"Although being married in Bora Bora sounds pretty nice."

"Yes it does," Aaron said, and then he glanced in the direction of the bedroom. "Now if you don't mind, I'm going to catch some shut-eye before we head out."

He left Reid to set up his bed on the couch and shut

the bedroom door behind him. Clara didn't say anything when he walked in, but her breathing didn't suggest she had fallen asleep yet.

***

The bed was barely big enough for the two of them, but Aaron knew that was all they needed. He intended to keep his arms firmly wrapped around Clara the entire night. Stripping down to his underwear, he climbed under the covers next to her warm body. She was still in his t-shirt, and the thought of her in it excited him.

She rolled over so that they were now facing each other. The full moon filtered through the small window, and he could just make out her features. He lightly touched her nose, her cheek, and ran his thumb across her lips.

"I love you, Aaron," she said in the dark.

Only twice before had Aaron heard those words from a woman in his bed, and it had been his cue to get as far away as possible. But not this time. They weren't even a surprise to him.

"I'm not going anywhere," he told her.

She kissed him with a ferocity that made Aaron's head spin. He slipped his hands under the t-shirt to glide up her smooth skin and discovered only hot bare flesh beneath it. The shirt needed to go now, he decided, and she didn't protest. Clara pushed him onto his back and proceeded to straddle his hips, letting the covers fall behind her. There was a smile on her face that he had never seen before, and he liked it. He reached up to touch her chest, and she took one of his hands, bringing it up to her mouth to suck on his fingers. Yes, this was definitely an undiscovered side of her. One he was ready to explore.

She bent down to kiss his mouth but didn't stay there for long. Soon her tongue was licking its way down his neck and to his chest. Her hips started to slide down his legs, and next thing he knew, she was at the foot of the bed pulling off his underwear. She placed a single knee between his legs and ran a hand up his thigh, stopping at the base of his shaft.

Oh god, was she about to do what he thought she was going to do? His question was answered by her warm mouth wrapping around him. Her tongue flicked across the tip and he knew she was playing with fire. Her hair felt like silk against his inner thighs.

"Oh, Clara," he moaned, and she briefly redoubled her efforts before stopping altogether. It was disappointing, but then she climbed up and slid down onto him, and it was the most wonderful feeling as she moved back and forth. Her hands rested on his chest and he took them into his, and she was gripping him so hard, he knew she had to be close. He could feel her whole body tensing around him as she moved faster and faster, biting her lip as a tiny sound escaped her, and he knew it was only a fraction of what she was keeping inside. She hadn't forgotten about Reid in the other room, even if *he* had.

Just as she started to slow down, Aaron rolled her onto her back and slipped a hand under her thigh, wrapping her leg around him.

He pounded even harder and buried his face into her delicious neck as he loomed nearer and nearer to the edge. Suddenly he could feel the wave of another orgasm taking grip of Clara's body, and he lost it with her.

***

Aaron's hand lightly traced Clara's spine as she laid across his chest listening to the steady rhythm of his beating heart. Her body was ready to succumb to sleep, but she fought it for fear of waking up in the morning to discover it was all a dream.

"Where should we go?" she asked.

"You should be getting some sleep," he said.

"I know. But I'm not ready yet. So where should we go?"

"Well, where would you like to go?" he asked.

"Can we really go anywhere?"

"I would suggest we avoid any big cities," he said. "But otherwise, yes, we can go anywhere."

"Where would *you* like to go?" she asked.

"Me?"

She lifted her head to look at him. The last trace of moonlight spilling into the room was just bright enough to make out the line of his jaw, the slope of his nose, even the length of his dark lashes.

"Yes," she said. "If you could choose anywhere, where would you go?"

She watched his mouth curl up into a smile.

"I'm happy with anywhere you are," he said.

"That's not an answer," she said, but smiled at his response.

"It's the truth."

"Have you traveled much before?"

"More than you can imagine. I've been to countries you've probably never even heard of."

It occurred to Clara there was so much she didn't know about Aaron. But she couldn't wait to learn it all.

"Was it dangerous?" she asked.

"You really are determined not to go to sleep, aren't you?"

"I'm worried I'll wake up and you'll be gone," she said.

His hand slid up to the base of her neck and he lifted his head to kiss her.

"I promise," he whispered, "I'm not going anywhere."

***

"Clara, honey, it's time to wake up."

Clara moaned and tried to open her eyes, but they just felt so heavy.

"Wake up, Clara, we need to get going."

She tried harder to open her eyes and slowly focused on Aaron's face inches from her own.

"What time is it?" she asked

"It's four-thirty," he said. "We should leave before the sun comes up."

No wonder it felt like she had only just closed her eyes.

"I promise you can sleep in the car once we're on the road."

"Got it," she muttered, sitting up in bed.

Aaron gestured to clothes at the foot of the bed. "I rummaged around and found some clothes that should fit if you didn't want to put the dress back on."

"Thanks," she said.

"There's food when you're ready."

"I'll be out in a minute."

She walked out of the bedroom wearing the black tank top and jeans that Aaron had procured.

"I think the jeans might be a bit tight," she said.

Aaron's face lit up when he looked at her. "I don't know, I think they might be a perfect fit."

Clara blushed but smiled at his approval. "They'll give in a few hours," she assured him.

The smell of bacon wafting from her plate on the table reminded Clara just how hungry she was. Her last meal was a distant memory.

"I'm afraid bacon and toast is the only thing we have to offer," said Reid, who was leaning against the counter with a mug of coffee. "Oh. And coffee." He raised his mug. "Care for some?"

"Coffee would be wonderful," she said and sat down at the table. It was hard not to shovel the food into her mouth as fast as possible.

"It's not very good," Reid said as he handed her a mug, "but it does the job."

"There's sugar and powdered creamer," Aaron said, pushing them across the table to her. "Provisions in these unmanned houses tend to be limited."

"It's fine," she said.

The second she drank the last drop, Aaron was ushering her out the door while Reid did a walk-through.

"What's he doing?" she asked from the back seat of the Charger. She was pretty sure she was going to need a nap soon, coffee or not.

"He's wiping down the place of prints," said Aaron. "Making sure there's no trace of us."

"Oh." He explained it all so calmly as though it were normal. But Clara found it unnerving. Was this what was in store for her? Would she ever get used to "leaving no trace?" No signs that she ever existed.

Reid jumped into the passenger seat. "We're good."

Aaron started the car and the glow of the dashboard lights became the only light source. Clara leaned her head against the window, staring at the blank sky as they pulled away from the cottage. The stars had tucked in for the night, but the sun had yet to make an appearance. She reflected on her own parting with the darkness of her past, but she was still waiting for the sun to rise. To face it with new hope and the promise of a brighter future. Her eyes closed and she let the hum of the road lull her.

CHAPTER NINE

It did not surprise Aaron one bit when Clara dozed off less than twenty minutes after getting back on the road. He had hated waking her so early, but it wasn't wise to stay in one place for too long. Until they were out of the country, neither would be getting any decent sleep. Once they were safe, he would let her sleep all day. Aaron imagined them on a beach somewhere napping together in the sun. A smile appeared on his face as he also pictured them tending to each other's sunburns.

"Do I even want to know what you're thinking about?" Reid asked from the passenger seat.

Aaron's smile grew even bigger. "No, you do not."

"It suits you," said Reid.

"What does?" Aaron asked.

"Being in love."

"I don't know what you're talking about," said Aaron.

"You're a horrible liar, Wells."

"I'm an excellent liar."

"Okay. But right now, you're not doing so well."

"Do you think I'm doing the right thing?" he asked Reid.

"I think I'm the wrong guy to be asking that," said Reid.

"You're the perfect guy to be asking. Was it worth it? Do you have any regrets?"

"Oh, it was worth it. No regrets whatsoever." Reid paused. "Well, save maybe one."

Aaron glanced at him.

"It almost cost me my best friend," said Reid. "But that being said, I still wouldn't have done anything different."

The sun was starting to tinge the sky as they drove east, but Aaron's mind was on Reid's words. He had no idea what was in store for him and Clara. But he was confident that as long as they were together, it was going to be all right. A little tricky at first, but all right. Reid had called it. He was in love.

***

Clara's eye fluttered open as the car pulled off an exit.

"What's going on?" she asked.

"Stopping for gas and provisions," Aaron said.

She pulled his jacket tighter around her and inhaled. It smelled like him and conjured images of last night, putting a smile on her face. And to think there was to be plenty more where that came from. In the light of day, her future was looking pretty bright indeed.

"I have to go pee," she said when they had stopped at a pump.

"Don't get out yet," said Aaron. "Let me grab a hat from the trunk." He popped the trunk before jumping out and she slipped the heels back onto her feet.

"Before I forget," Reid said, twisting to face her. "I found this on the coffee table and wasn't sure if you still wanted it."

The pearl bracelet was in his hand and Clara scowled at it.

"I suppose I could pawn it," she said, taking it from him. "I'm sure we'll be able to use the cash."

Aaron opened the passenger door and the bracelet was carelessly dropped onto the seat.

"This should keep your face off any security cameras," he said, placing a plain black cap low over her brow. "Just be sure to keep your eyes low."

Clara frowned. "No trace, right?"

"Afraid so. But I have to say you look pretty damn cute in my hat."

This put a smile on her face, and Aaron brushed

her cheek. "Now come on. You'll need the bathroom key."

He took her hand in his and they walked into the gas station while Reid started pumping gas.

"Any special requests?" Aaron asked.

"I'm fine with whatever." She looked around the store, trying to keep her eyes low as Aaron had instructed, and saw sweatshirts hanging from a rack in the far corner. "Will you grab a sweatshirt and maybe some flip flops so I don't have to wear these heels the whole time?"

"Will do."

She gave him a peck on the lips, grabbed the key from the clerk, and walked back out to the restroom at the back of the building.

The bathroom had seen better days, but Clara had seen worse bathrooms. She peed as quickly as she could and was washing her hands when there was a knock at the door.

"I'll be right out," she shouted.

Clara dried her hands, used the paper towel to open the door, and came face to face with Sergio. And then everything went black.

***

When Reid had finished filling the tank, Aaron had the clerk ring everything up. He walked out with two plastic bags full of goodies.

"You driving?" Reid asked.

"I thought it would be your turn," said Aaron. "Where's Clara?"

"In the bathroom."

"Still?" It didn't feel right to Aaron. He handed Reid the bags. "Put these in the car, will ya?"

He walked towards the bathroom and rounded the corner in time to see Clara's limp body being poured into a black sedan.

"Hey!" he shouted, now running towards the vehicle. The door slammed shut and the vehicle sped off. Aaron changed direction back to the Charger ,where Reid was already in the driver's seat.

"They've got Clara," he shouted as the sedan peeled out of the driveway right in front of them. He jumped into the passenger seat and Reid, who already had the engine roaring, started driving before Aaron had even shut the door.

"You're sure that's her?" Reid asked.

"Yes, I'm sure!" Aaron said as he pulled a gun from the glove box. "I just watched them take her! Where the hell were you?"

"I was getting gas," said Reid, closing in on the sedan. "I didn't think—how did they find her so fast?"

"Hell if I know. Get closer!" He rolled the window down and prepared to shoot through it when shots were fired back at him and he ducked. "Dammit."

Suddenly the car was slammed from behind.

"What the fuck?" yelled Reid, glancing in the rear-view mirror.

Aaron turned and saw a second black sedan on their tail. Shots fired from it as well, and both men crouched down in their seats as the back window shattered.

"Stay low and don't lose that car," Aaron said while he climbed into the back seat.

Chunks of broken glass were still hanging on, and he punched these out to get a better shot at the rear vehicle. A couple bullets to the driver side of its front window sent the car into a spin. But it wasn't out for the count, and Aaron watched as the driver was pushed out the door and someone else put the car back on the road.

Aaron turned to Reid. "We need to stop that car before the other one catches up!"

Reid slammed into the back corner of the sedan with Clara and it swerved, but corrected itself quickly. More shots fired at them, and this time the car slowed until it was even with the Charger, where a well-aimed tap from the sedan sent the Charger into the ditch, causing the engine to stall. The second car caught up and fired a barrage of bullets as it went by. Reid and Aaron scrambled out of the passenger door as quickly as they could and emptied their clips, but both cars were out of sight.

"Fuck!" Aaron shouted. "FUCK! I promised her."

His balled a fist in his hair. "I told her he would never hurt her again and I couldn't even give her twenty-four god damn hours!" He crouched down to put his head between his knees, on the brink of tears. There was no way of knowing where she was going now, or what Morozov was going to do to her. He assumed she'd still been alive when they took her, otherwise they would have just left her body. But how much longer did she have?

"How the hell did they find her?" Aaron asked, standing up. "We weren't followed, and she had nothing on her. Nothing!" He slammed the car roof.

Reid pulled something from the floor of the back seat. "Not nothing," he said. "She was wearing this when we picked her up."

Aaron took the pearl bracelet from Reid. Over the clasp was a band of onyx. He pried it off and discovered it had been carved out and inside was a small tracking chip.

Aaron scowled and wound up his arm, ready to throw the bracelet as far away as possible, when Reid stopped him.

"Wait," he said. "If that's how they found her, I might be able to trace the signal. It could lead us back to her."

Aaron looked at the jewelry in his hand. It was the only hope they had.

"Hurry up," he said, handing it back to Reid.

***

"Clara, my love, time to wake up," said a distant voice.

Didn't Aaron already wake me up? thought Clara.

"Clara, wake up." The voice sounded much closer now, and it didn't sound anything like Aaron. It sounded like….

"Clara!"

Her eyes flew open and she was face to face with Aleksandr, who looked angrier than she had ever seen him.

"Ah ,good. You're awake," he said. "I wanted you to witness this."

Her knees were pressing against something hard, and she realized she was on them with someone holding her arms behind her back. And the side of her head throbbed like someone had punched her. Wait, did Sergio punch her? She dropped her head as she remembered opening the door of the bathroom, but Aleksandr grabbed a fistful of her hair, sending waves of fire through her brain, and forced her to look at something.

"See what you have done to yet another one of my men?" he said.

Sergio, who only moments ago (to her at least) had looked so smug as he raised a fist to her face, was now hanging from a chain in the middle of the empty warehouse. Or rather, she was pretty sure it was

Sergio. His face was so bloody and swollen she couldn't be sure. He coughed, sending blood spraying in their direction. He wasn't dead. Yet.

"How is this my fault?" she asked, and Aleksandr's response was to smack her across the face. She tasted blood and knew the cut from yesterday had reopened.

"Just like Ryan," he said, "Sergio had one job. To keep you safe. And just like Ryan, he failed."

"I don't know, I was pretty safe before you came along today." Another slap. Clara knew she should probably learn to keep her mouth shut, but for the first time in her life, she was taking pleasure in pissing Aleksandr off. A little fun before she bit the bullet.

"If he had failed, why did you send him to take me?" she asked.

"It was supposed to be his chance to redeem himself," he said, walking over to where Sergio was hanging. "But he wasn't supposed to hit you." He punched Sergio in the gut, and more blood sprayed from his mouth, barely missing Aleksandr. He always knew how to land a punch without getting dirty.

"You hear that, boys?" Clara said. "Only Aleksandr is allowed to beat me to a bloody pulp."

He was in front her at once, placing his hands around her neck. "Do you think this is funny?"

"Just kill me now," she said. "Get it over with."

"No."

"No?" She was confused. "Why not?"

"Because I love you."

She forced a laugh. "Now *that* is funny." This time she took the punch to the gut.

"Tie her up in the office," he said.

The man on Clara's right pulled her off the floor and threw her over his shoulder.

"Make sure you don't hurt me though," she said, still gasping for breath.

"Give me your gun," she heard Aleksandr ask someone. The next sound was a shot she was sure went right to Sergio's head. Another little piece of her died with him. Of course Aleksandr wasn't going to kill her anytime soon. Doing it little by little would be much more enjoyable for him.

***

The car had been fixed and was ready to go—they just needed to know where. Aaron was pacing behind Reid, who had the computer and tracking chip spread out on the trunk of the car.

"Breathing down my neck isn't going to make me work any faster," said Reid.

"And I doubt it's going to make you work any slower either," Aaron said. "The longer we wait to move, the farther away she gets."

"I think you might be wrong."

Aaron glared at him. "Sorry?"

"Because I've pinpointed where the signal was being sent, and it's not moving. Judging by this map, they're in a warehouse about ten miles from here."

"Good man." Aaron slapped him on the back. "Let's go."

***

The office Clara had been tied up in was a mostly empty room at the back of a warehouse containing nothing but an old metal desk and two chairs, one of which she was bound to. Another backroom. She was really starting to hate "back rooms."

Aleksandr came in with an ice pack in his hand and positioned the second chair directly in front of her before sitting down. He pressed the ice to her left cheek and the cold felt good against the throbbing pain.

"Why do you always force my hand, Clara?" he asked.

"Slow learner, I guess," she said. "Maybe I took one too many to the head."

"Still with the jokes. You're not funny, you know. Now tell me who those men were."

"What does it matter?" she asked.

He raised his hand to strike her and she braced for it, but the blow never came.

"See," he said, "there you go again. Just answer my question and I won't have to hurt you."

[144]

"Then I guess you're going to have to hurt me."

She could see the turmoil in his eyes. What was stopping him?

"When did you stop loving me?" he asked, and the question hit her in the heart.

"What?"

He pulled out his phone and pulled up some pictures.

"Do you remember these?" he said, swiping through photos from their honeymoon only three years ago. He held up a self-taken shot of him on the beach, with her kissing his cheek, and a tear rolled down her face.

"How did we go from this to," he gestured at her, "*this?*"

"I stopped loving you the day you threw me up against the wall," she said. "And I started hating you with a vengeance the night you killed our child."

Pain spread across his face. "I am sorry for that. If I had known….That hurt me as well."

She shook her head at him.

"But that doesn't mean it's too late to start over," he said. "We can still be a family. There's still hope for us."

She kept shaking her head. "No, no, NO! That's where you're wrong!" Fury swept over her. "There is no hope for us, and there is no family in our future. Even if I could have another child, I would never have one with you!"

"Even if you could?" he said. "What do you mean by—"

"You broke me, you bastard!" she screamed. "When you threw me down the stairs you not only killed my baby, you caused too much damage! I will never have children!"

He leapt from his chair, forming words with his mouth, but no sounds came out. He circled the room, then came back and gripped the back of the chair. His knuckles were turning white, and suddenly he picked up the chair and slammed it against the desk.

"When were you going to tell me?" he shouted into her face. She could feel the heat of his breath against her cheek as she turned away from him.

She was still trying to form an answer when gunshots echoed out in the warehouse.

"What the hell?" Aleksandr asked, spinning around.

He walked out and Clara could hear yelling before Aleksandr came running back in, a gun in hand, and started untying her.

He was cursing in Ukrainian as he he dragged her out of the room with the gun on her, and it didn't take long for Clara to read the situation. Aaron and Reid had arrived.

***

It was unlikely that Morozov knew Reid would

reverse trace the signal on the bracelet, which gave them the element of surprise. But that went out the window after the first shot was fired.

The first man, the door guard, had been easy enough to take out. Problem was, they didn't know there was a second man coming around the corner. He had been mid-puff on a cigarette when he caught sight of them, and Reid was able to get off a shot before the man had a finger on his trigger.

Aaron opened the door a crack and was met with guns pointed in his direction. He immediately closed the door and a couple bullets made it through the thin metal.

"We need another entrance," he told Reid.

"You go around," said Reid. "I'll try and distract them here."

"I think I made out four men," said Aaron.

"Clara?"

Aaron shook his head. "No Morozov either."

He took off in the direction the smoking man had come from, and as he rounded the building, he found Morozov trying to force Clara into the same sedan that had peeled off earlier.

"Morozov!" he shouted.

They both paused to look up, then Clara fought Morozov even harder.

Aaron shot out one of the car tires just as another gunman exited a door, and after a quick survey of the situation, started firing at him. Aaron was able to duck back around the corner just in time, but when he looked back around, Clara and Morozov were gone. Knowing that the car wouldn't get far with a flat tire, he must have dragged her back inside.

The other gunman was still shooting past the corner that Aaron was using for cover, a couple bullets blasting into the cement wall. There was a break and Aaron didn't waste the opportunity. In one shot he was able to get the guy right in the chest.

Keeping an eye out for any other assailants, Aaron entered the building. It was relatively small but open, which he knew could be bad or good. The only sound was Clara, but it was hard to tell what her condition was. Following the muffled noise, he tracked them to a corner where Morozov was using Clara as a shield, a gun pressed to her temple. A body hung from chains nearby, and as Aaron glanced at it, he caught movement along the rafters. Since he hadn't been shot yet, Aaron had to assume it was Reid.

"Toss your gun," Morozov shouted as him.

Aaron said nothing and kept his weapon aimed in their direction.

"I said toss your gun!" Morozov screamed, pressing the pistol harder into Clara.

Aaron put a hand up and gently placed it on the ground.

"Now kick it over."

Aaron kicked it so that it only covered half the distance between them, but that was still twenty feet away.

"It's over Morozov. Why don't you just let Clara go?"

Aleksandr laughed. "That's not going to happen. It's over when I say it's over and I know you won't risk hurting her. Not beautiful Clara." He kissed her ear and she struggled against him.

"Shooting me won't solve anything. I've got another man here and he won't let you leave. With or without Clara. I'm the only one here who might let you walk. But only if you let Clara go."

"She's mine, or she's dead!" He shouted.

And then Aaron saw the determination in Clara's face, the rage burning in her eyes.

"Clara! No!" He watched in horror as her left hand grabbed Aleksandr's gun hand and tried to slam it into the wall behind them. It must have been enough to catch him off guard because the gun flew from his grip and both he and Clara scrambled for it.

"Jackson!" Aaron called out.

"I don't have a clear shot!" he yelled down.

"Damn it!" Aaron ran towards them, picking up his gun along the way. He was only a couple steps from being able to pull Morozov off of her when a shot rang out, and Aaron froze both bodies went limp.

***

The gun went off, and Clara froze. She felt the warm blood oozing across her chest, but no pain. Was this how it felt to die? Except there *was* pain, it just wasn't coming from her chest. Only her head and her shoulder blades pressing into the hard concrete hurt.

"Clara," said Aaron from somewhere nearby. His voice was quiet and scared.

For the first time, she realized Aleksandr wasn't moving either. It was his weight on her that was pushing her back into the ground.

"Aaron," she called out. Aleksandr was lifted off her and she saw Aaron's relieved expression.

"You're not shot?" he asked.

"I don't think so." She held her bloodied hands to her face for a better look. Aleksandr's blood on her hands. Looking over, she saw the anger, forever frozen on his face.

"Are you all right?" asked Aaron.

She started to nod, but suddenly she was rolling onto all fours and watched as what little she had eaten that day was vomited onto the concrete. When that was gone, it was clear liquid. Her stomach just kept heaving like it would never stop.

Aaron pulled her hair back to keep it out of the mess in front of her. She heard footsteps approach, and a rag was being handed to her when at last nothing else came up. She felt Aaron's arms pull her into him, and she began sobbing into his chest.

"It's over," Aaron said, rubbing her back. "It's all over."

CHAPTER TEN

Clara was balled up in the back of the Charger wearing the sweatshirt Aaron had picked up at the gas station. Her throat burned, and she could smell faint traces of vomit in her hair despite Aaron's effort. She was also wondering why they weren't driving as far away as possible from this hell-hole already.

She stared out the window at Aaron and Reid who were in an animated discussion by the warehouse entrance. A lot of nodding and head shaking. Reid even got on his phone and Aaron looked over to give her a sympathetic smile.

After what felt like an eternity, they walked over, but only Aaron climbed into the back seat with her while Reid stayed outside the vehicle.

"How are you doing?" he asked.

"I've been better," she said. "But I will be better."

"Yes, you will."

"What's going on?" she asked. "Why aren't we leaving?"

"We need to talk," he said.

"It's over, isn't it?" Panic was rising in her voice. "We can do whatever we want."

"I wish it were that simple. But I'm still in a lot of trouble."

"So we go on the run as planned," she said. "At least now we won't have to worry about Aleksandr anymore."

"But you don't need to go on the run anymore."

"What are you saying?" She choked back tears. "You said you weren't going anywhere."

He tried to pull her into his arms but she pushed him away. "You promised!"

"It's only temporary," he said. "Just hear me out."

Clara's arms crossed her chest and she kept a distance between them.

"If you leave, it could look bad. But if you stay here and tell them what happened, there is no reason to believe it wasn't self-defense. We'll call the cops and we'll call Agent Maxwell, my supervisor. You will have to go home and make some statements."

"I can't go home," she said, shuddering. "His family is there; it won't be safe."

"It will be. Reid is going to meet you up there, and he'll make sure you're safe."

"But not you."

"But not me," he said. "Which kills me."

"Will I ever see you again?"

"Absolutely. That's why I can't go home with you. I risk jail time and then who knows when I would see you again. I'm going to go into hiding. When the time is right, when things have settled down, you will join me. If you want to."

Clara closed the gap and wrapped her arms around him. "Of course I want to. But does it have to be so long? Can't we just go now?"

"No point in us both being fugitives," he said into her ear.

She pulled away from him with tears starting to trickle down her cheeks, and he wiped them away.

"It'll be okay," he said.

"I don't know if I can go through this alone."

"I know. Jillian, Reid's girlfriend, is on her way. She's going to be at your side the whole time. Then she and Reid will be with you in Seattle until it's safe."

She nodded. "How long until she gets here?"

"About an hour."

"Will you just sit here with me until then?"

"Of course."

***

Clara had passed out in Aaron's arms and was breathing softly when he heard the motorcycle telling him Jillian had arrived. But he wasn't ready to wake Clara, wasn't ready to say goodbye. Someone tapped on the window, and he knew it was Reid signaling it was time. He closed his eyes, took a deep breath, and tried to find his voice.

"Clara, honey," he said, choking on the words.

She responded by burrowing deeper into him, and he had to fight back the tears.

"Jillian's here, Clara. It's time."

There was a pleasant sleepy expression on her face when she finally sat up, and then Aaron watched as reality replaced it, and he tried to remind himself this was only temporary. They would be together soon. But he hated knowing he wasn't going to be by her side during the next few weeks when things would be rough.

As he helped her out of the car, Aaron saw a resolve set into her face. This was Clara the Fighter. The woman that would do whatever needed to be done, whether she liked it or not. This was the woman he had fallen in love with.

***

It was all Clara could do not to fall apart as she walked hand-in-hand with Aaron to where Reid was standing with a dark-haired girl next to a red motorcycle.

"You must be Clara," said Reid's girlfriend.

Clara nodded.

"Well, I'm Jillian, as you've probably guessed, and I'm going to help you get through this."

"Okay."

Aaron's hand gave her a squeeze.

"You two should probably get out of here," said Jillian.

Both men turned to their partners.

"I'm sure she'll tell you all about it," said Aaron, "but Jillian has been through something similar, so she really can help you get through this."

Clara nodded again, not trusting herself to speak.

"And Reid will be waiting when you get to Seattle. You won't be alone."

"I know," she said. "I just wish you could be with me."

"I will be. I promise to send for you when this is all over."

Aaron held her face, and she stared deep into his big brown eyes searching hers.

"I love you, Clara, and I wouldn't leave you with these two if I didn't think they could keep you safe."

A single tear finally broke free, and Aaron wiped it with his thumb before pressing his mouth against her. God he tasted good. His smell, his touch…she wondered how long it would be until she knew it all again. Weeks? Months?

All too soon Aaron was pushing her away. Jillian's arm appeared around her shoulder and the two watched as Reid and Aaron climbed on the bike Jillian had arrived on and sped off.

"Does it ever get easier?" Clara asked.

"Does what get easier?"

"Saying goodbye."

Jillian sighed. "Nope."

"Now what?" said Clara.

"We wait. Reid said Aaron wanted get out of town before he called this in." Jillian moved over to a step and sat down. "I'm sure it won't be long. These government agencies tend to act pretty fast when the shit hits the fan."

Clara sat down next to Jillian. And they waited.

***

About a mile out of town, Aaron tapped Reid, signaling him to pull over. When the bike stopped, Aaron climbed off and dug out his cell phone for one last call.

"Wells?" Gavin answered on the other end. "Where the hell are you?"

"Aleksandr Morozov is dead," he told him.

"Morozov is dead? What the fuck did you do, Wells?"

"It wasn't me," said Aaron. "Clara Morozov shot him."

"His *wife?*"

"I told you she wanted out."

"Shit," said Gavin. "Are you with her?"

"No. She and the body are at an abandoned warehouse just east of the Colorado state line off of I-70."

"Then where are you?"

"That depends," he said. "What happens when I come in?"

"Well *that* depends on whether or not you had anything to do with this."

Aaron didn't say anything.

"Did you?" Gavin asked.

"Maybe."

"Then *maybe* you violated a direct order, and that won't be taken lightly."

"I'm not coming in unless you can guarantee I walk," said Aaron.

"I can't make any guarantees until I know what kind of cluster fuck you're leaving me to clean up."

"Then talk to me when you do know."

"Wait, how do I—"

Aaron hung up the phone, texted Clara's exact location to Gavin, then smashed his phone into the pavement.

"A bit over dramatic, don't you think?" said Reid. "Just leave the phone behind."

"I know," said Aaron. "But it felt good."

"Hop on," Reid said, handing him his helmet. "Time to get you to a bus station."

***

Jillian was right—it didn't take long for them to show up. Within in an hour, the place was crawling with suits and uniformed agents.

At first they were told to remain where they were, and for the next hour they watched as the few men still alive and zip-tied were loaded into the back of unmarked cars. Then they started hauling away the bodies. Clara felt queasy again as Aleksandr's body went by. For all the times she dreamed of this day, it was still hard to believe that he, who had always been larger than life, was now lying dead on that gurney. It was difficult to wrap her head around.

A new vehicle arrived and a tall, dark man in aviators stepped out and walked purposefully in their direction. This was clearly the man in charge, Clara decided.

"You must be Clara Morozov," he said, removing his sunglasses to reveal hazel eyes.

She nodded.

"And Jillian Sandro," he said with a sigh. "I had hoped I would never see you again."

"Good to see you too, Agent Maxwell," said Jillian.

"Should I even bother asking if Jackson is here?" he asked, scanning the scene.

"Nope," she told him.

"Riker!" he barked to another agent, and the man came rushing over.

"I want you to give this man a statement of

[159]

everything that happened from the moment you left Seattle," he said to Clara. "I'll go over it and see if I have any questions."

She nodded and Agent Maxwell marched off, barking more orders as everyone tried to process the scene. She did not envy his job one bit.

***

It felt like anything but home sweet home when Clara walked into her house the next day with Jillian and Reid, who had met them at the airport.

"This place is gorgeous," Jillian said as she descended the stairs into the living room. She turned around and Clara saw the regret on her face. "I'm sorry."

"No, it's fine," said Clara. "It *is* beautiful. It just holds a lot of ugly memories."

"Where would you like me to put my stuff?" Jillian asked, holding the single backpack she had traveled with.

"I—I'm not sure." It didn't feel right to put Jillian up in the room Ryan had always used when he stayed over.

"You know what, it's fine. I can just set it here for now." She placed it next to the couch. "No rush."

Clara realized she didn't even want to sleep in her own room. Everything started to spin, so she sat in a nearby chair.

Jillian rushed over. "Reid, why don't you go get

some water."

"I'm fine," said Clara.

"I know," said Jillian, "But have some water anyway."

She took the glass from Reid and drank it.

"You should probably eat something too," he said.

Clara knew he was right, but she didn't know if she could manage it.

"Tell you what," said Jillian. "Why don't you go up and take a shower while I fix us some dinner?"

"That would be nice," she said. If nothing else she wouldn't have to watch them handle her with kid gloves.

The first thing Clara saw when she walked into the master bedroom was the gaudy wedding portrait. Aleksandr's smiling face stared down at her. At first she was sad. All that hope and promise. And naiveté. And then she was pissed. He was the one who had held the carrot out for her. Didn't tell her that her dreams came at a very costly price. Had waited until they were married to reveal his true nature.

Clara tried to take the portrait off the wall, but it resisted.

"Aaarrggghh!" she growled as she tugged with all her might until it ripped from the wall.

Reid and Jillian appeared in the doorway just in time to see her smash it against the dresser.

Satisfied, she looked up to see the fear tinged with

concern in their faces.

"Just doing a little redecorating," she told them.

Jillian's hand clasped over her mouth, but Reid was focusing on something behind her.

Clara turned around and saw the safe. "The safe," she said. Was Aleksandr's gun in there? She vaguely recalled him asking to use someone's gun when he shot Sergio, which meant he never had it with him in Vegas.

"I have a question for you, Reid," she said.

"What's that?"

"If the agency had access to some of Aleksandr's personal items, do you think it would help take down other members of his organization?"

"I would imagine so," he said.

"Because behind this safe is the gun he used, along with some other documents that I'm sure contain sensitive information."

"Do you know the code?"

"No, but I'm sure we can find a safe cracker."

**

The suits were back, scouring the house while Clara sat in the den, mindlessly watching the news. Jillian sat nearby, flipping through a magazine. There was no mention of her husband—not that Clara was surprised. She imagined the agency wanted to keep this thing quiet, and it might be a few days before they spun a tale that was worthy of the news outlets.

Aleksandr Morozov would be missed by *some* people, wouldn't he? She just hoped they could leave out the part about her being responsible for his death. Being his widow was going to be stigma enough. Clara wondered how soon she could go back to her maiden name.

She was losing interest in the television when a story caught her attention.

"And in other news," the anchor woman announced, "a local man was killed in a tragic auto accident last night just outside of Las Vegas."

"I know him," Clara said, pushing the pause button on a picture of Tristan Brandt.

Jillian looked up. "You know him?" she asked in disbelief.

"Well, I met him a couple times. I'm pretty sure he was working with Aleksandr on something."

"Reid?" Jillian called out. "Reid!"

"What is it?" Clara asked.

Reid walked in. "What's going on?"

"That's the man," Jillian said. "The one on the boat."

"What are you talking about?" asked Reid.

"You've met him?" asked Clara.

"When I was abducted and Casimir took me to the boat, he was on it," said Jillian.

"Are you sure?" Reid asked.

"Yes! And now Clara just said that she thinks

Morozov was working with him."

"That would make sense if he was on Morozov's boat." Reid turned to Clara. "What do you know about him?"

"Not much. He claimed to be an art dealer, even owns a gallery in downtown Seattle. But I first met him in the back room of the restaurant, which rarely means something good."

"Do you have any idea what they may have been up to?"

She shook her head. "But they said he was just killed outside of Las Vegas. *We* were just in Vegas. That can't be a coincidence."

"I agree," said Reid. "I need to talk to Maxwell."

Reid was almost in the next room when Clara remembered something else.

"He had a girlfriend."

Reid turned back around.

"I only met her briefly at his gallery. Sadie? No wait, Sydney. Sydney Holden, I think."

Reid nodded and left to find Maxwell.

"What do you think this means?" Clara asked Jillian, but she just shrugged.

***

Maxwell and his agents had spent the whole afternoon clearing the house of anything that may have been Aleksandr's, and all Clara had said was "good riddance" to it all. She was told that it would take some time to figure out the Brandt connection, and even then, it was unlikely she would be privy to that information. Again, Clara didn't really care. Her husband was dead, never to touch her again, and soon she would be able to start a whole new life.

Reid and Jillian had turned in for the night in one of the guest rooms, and after Clara tried unsuccessfully to fall asleep in one of the other guest rooms, she went into the kitchen and grabbed the most expensive bottle of wine she could find.

The cool air felt good on her face as she moved out onto the balcony where a few boats were still twinkling across Lake Washington in the late hour.

She was halfway through her second glass when Jillian walked out, sporting her own wine glass.

"Can't sleep?" she asked, pouring from the bottle.

"No," said Clara. "Every time I close my eyes, I just see Aleksandr's face."

"It will get better, I promise."

"How did you get through it?" Clara asked.

"Reid," said Jillian. "He was the only one that could possibly understand what I was going through."

God, Clara missed Aaron.

"He'll be back soon enough," Jillian said, reading her thoughts. "But until then, know that you can talk to me anytime."

"Thank you," said Clara.

Even though nothing else was said, Jillian's presence was a comfort as they sat in silence, sipping their wine.

***

Two weeks later and there was nothing keeping Clara in Washington any longer. Maxwell had gotten everything he could from her and had managed to capture any of Aleksandr's men who hadn't gone into hiding yet, including Dimitre Morozov. Clara secretly hoped he died of a heart attack before the trial.

With all the evidence they had acquired, it wasn't going to be necessary for her to testify. So here she was at Sea-Tac International Airport, waiting with Reid and Jillian to board a flight to Denver. It had been their idea, and Clara couldn't think of any reason why not.

It turned out there had been quite a few legitimate assets that would have gone to Clara, but she instructed the lawyer to liquidate them all and donate the money to Seattle Children's Hospital. It would be a generous sum, and she saw a new wing in their future, but she asked that the donation be made anonymously. They would have to find someone else to name it after.

Everything she had wanted to keep was packed in her carry-on bag, and she had an envelope of cash that should be just enough to help her make a fresh start in Denver.

Jillian started giggling over something Reid had said and it brought Clara back into the present. Seeing them together and the bond they shared made Clara's heart ache for Aaron. There had still been no word, but she was sure she would hear from him soon enough now that everything had settled.

Now we wait.

***

Aaron's knee bounced up and down as he sat in an airport terminal. His own flight had arrived into the same terminal two hours ago, and now the plane he'd been waiting for had finally pulled into the gate. He jumped out of his seat as they opened the jetway doors.

It felt like ages before people started coming out. And then he saw Clara. She was laughing and it was the most beautiful thing he had ever seen. Their eyes met, and it didn't register at first. She glanced away, then back at him, and her eyes went huge. Aaron's face broke into a grin and she was running past people right into his arms. He caught her and hugged her so hard her feet lifted off the ground.

"Oh, Clara," he whispered into her ear.

"You're here," she said as he set her down. "I'm not imagining this, am I?"

He looked down into her bright green eyes. "Yes, I'm really here."

"Did I forget to tell you he'd be meeting us here?"

Reid said, pulling the carry-on she had ditched.

Clara punched him. "Yeah, I think you did."

Both men laughed.

"I told him not to tell you," said Aaron. "I wanted it to be a surprise."

Clara looked at Jillian, who shook her head. "I had no idea either."

She turned back to him. "Well, it's the best surprise ever."

Aaron put his arm around her and the four found their way out of the terminal.

"But how are you here?" she asked. "Are you not in trouble anymore?"

"The bosses decided the operation wasn't a complete bust," he said.

"Aleksandr is dead and they caught most of his men," she said. "I'd say that it was a success."

"That's my Clara," Aaron said as he kissed the top of her head. "So they decided that, no, I'm not in trouble. I'm also no longer welcome at the agency and have been stripped of all clearance.

"That's not fair," said Jillian. "Why did Reid only get a slap on the wrist and then they tell you to fuck off?"

Everyone laughed at her candor.

"My record was not as squeaky clean as Saint Reid's here," said Aaron.

"Whatever," Reid muttered.

"What are you going to do now?" Clara asked as they got in line for a taxi.

He tucked her hair behind her ear and spoke softly. "I don't know, but I thought we'd figure it out together."

CHAPTER ELEVEN

Gavin Maxwell sat across from Anton Casimir, who was looking pretty smug for a guy in shackles. Gavin wondered if he would still be feeling that way by the end of their conversation.

"Ah," said Casimir. "Another agent looking for information, I see. Still trying to figure out who my buyer is?"

"Who is Tristan Brandt?" Gavin asked and watched the smirk disappear from Casimir's face, if only for a second, and his face started to go red.

"He was your buyer." Gavin said, hiding his own surprise. Without Casimir's reaction, he never would have suspected.

"Who is he?" Gavin asked again. "Why had we not heard of him before?"

"Tristan Brandt is a ghost. I doubt that's even his

real name." Then Casimir cocked his head. "Why are you not asking him these questions?"

"Because Tristan Brandt died in a car crash in Las Vegas last month."

"Brandt killed in an automobile accident," Casimir laughed. "Very unlikely."

"Dental records and DNA prove it was his body."

Casimir shrugged. Did he know something Gavin didn't?

"Perhaps you're right," said Gavin. "I mean, it does seem very suspicious that Brandt dies in a tragic accident only one day after Aleksandr Morozov was shot and killed."

Casimir laughed, but Gavin could tell it was forced. "Who could possibly get close enough to my cousin to shoot him?" he asked.

"His wife."

"That little bitch," Casimir said with a sneer. "I knew Dimitre should never have let him marry an outsider." Then he sighed. "If everyone is dead, then what do you need from me?"

"Tell me what else Brandt was involved in. What was he planning to do with the module and codes? Was he planning on using them himself?"

"As I said to the last agent who was here, what can you offer me? I think we both know I will never be leaving this place."

"True," said Gavin. "But we could make life a little

more pleasant in here for you. A little more fresh air, some additional amenities perhaps." Now that Casimir had been on McNeil Island for several months, he might be more willing to bargain. "Or I could make things less comfortable for you. The choice is yours."

Casimir pulled a slip of paper from his pocket and slid it across the table towards Gavin.

"You have a list already," said Gavin.

"I knew it was the only bargaining chip you had," he said.

Gavin looked over the list. All the items were within reason. Casimir must really hate it in here if he wasn't willing to risk it all by asking for the moon.

"I should be able to make this happen," said Gavin. "Now tell me what you know about Tristan Brandt."

"He runs a black market website," Casimir told him.

"You mean like Silk Road?"

"Exactly. The module would have gone up for bid, but it was worthless without the codes. That's where I came in."

"Had you worked with Brandt before?"

Casimir shook his head. "Morozov did though. He often provided Brandt with inventory; guns, girls, whatever would bring in money. But the kidnapping was more my line of work, so Morozov called me to help.

"And what do you know about his girlfriend, Sydney Holden?"

"I knew he had a girl, but I never met her or knew her name."

"So you don't know if she was working with him?"

"I don't think she was, but I do not know for sure."

Gavin stared at Casimir's list in his hand, trying to think of any other questions he should be asking. Finally he stood and gave a nod to the guard outside the door.

"Anything else you think I should know?" Gavin asked before walking out the door.

Casimir gave a slow, sinister smile. "Don't be surprised if Brandt isn't really dead."

Don't Miss

Ghost Lies

The Third Book in the Love & Lies Series

When Sydney Holden becomes the target of a man she thought was dead, Agent Maxwell may be the only person who can help her, if only she can trust him.

Available July 2015

Also available by Alex Strong

CrossFire: Love & Lies Book 1

Island Runaway

Acknowledgments

Thank you to all the people who have helped me get to this point; my husband and kids for accepting that mommy is busy right now without too much complaint, all my friends for letting me ramble on about book stuff, and my community for supporting me in ways that make my heart swell. For this book specifically I want to thank Cattigan for being such a kick-ass beta reader and my go-to marketing person. Thank you also to my editor Carrie O. for all your work on this book, and in the middle of a move no less! You've done an awesome job, I'm excited to work with you on more projects. And I can't let another opportunity go by without acknowledging my parents' influence. My mother was such an avid reader and I rarely saw her without a book in hand of variety of genres. I discovered more than one author after picking up a paperback she had left laying around. And my dad for always encouraging my storytelling abilities. No matter how out there the tale was, he never stopped me from telling them around the campfire.

About the Author

Alex Strong has loved stories, whether she's reading or telling them, since she was very young. But it wasn't until after the birth of her youngest son that she realized what she wanted to do most was be an author. Her past lives include working as a waitress, a sales clerk, and a nanny. Though she has been all around the world, including two years living in the Philippines as a child, Alex is proud to call the Pacific Northwest her home and lives in the Seattle suburbs with her husband, their two boys, and two fluffy dogs.

Stay in Touch

AlexStrongWrites.com
Facebook.com/AlexStrongWrites
@TheAlex_Strong